Lessons with Dad

by
Vicky Turrell

Vicky

Published by Leaf by Leaf Press 2021
www.leafbyleafpress.com

Copyright © Vicky Turrell 2021

Vicky Turrell has asserted her right to be identified as the author
of this work in accordance with the Copyright, Design and
Patents Act 1988

ISBN 978-1-9993122-5-1

Cover Photo by Unsplash
Cover Design by Branding by G
Printed and bound by Clays Ltd, Elocograf S.p.A.

Children are innately wise and realistic (after A.S. Neill)

Acknowledgements

I would like to thank the members of Oswestry Writers Group for all their encouragement especially during the pandemic lockdown when we could not meet.

I am greatly indebted to the members of Leaf by Leaf Press for their unwavering support and time. My thanks go to John Heap who has prepared my story for printing and Kirstie Edwards who helped me professionally.

Helen Baggott edited my story as she did with my previous two stories.

G Sabini-Roberts (Branding By G) has helped me devise the book cover and title. I wish to thank her for all her expertise and patience.

Lastly, thank you to all the members of my family who have supported me with the idea of creating of this book and bearing with me when I undertook the challenge and excitement of writing this story.

Lessons with Dad

by
Vicky Turrell

Introduction

My mother died a millionaire's death. Not that she ever was a millionaire, nor my father either come to that. They had worked all their lives, hard physical work, on their farm, with hardly a break. Then, when he was sixty-five, Dad retired and lived off his 'old age pension'.

They were used to getting up early to milk the cows and they did not see any reason to change the habit, even though they had been retired for many years.

They had a little routine. Not the rushed dressing into work clothes and gulping a cup of tea routine, but a predictable gentle series of events.

"Are you awake, Herb?"

"Yes."

He switched the radio on, and they listened to the farming programme in silence. Then they got up and got dressed. They took turns in the bathroom and Dad cooked bacon and eggs for breakfast. Then Mam went to sit in her favourite chair. Then Dad went into the kitchen to make a pot of tea. Then Mam died.

Dad was still in the kitchen pouring their morning tea, he came back with two cups. We went over the events so many times afterwards, hardly able to believe what had happened, it was so shocking for us. But Mam died peacefully, at home, sitting in her own chair with all the familiar sounds around her.

My two sisters lived not too far away so they were able to call and help, when necessary, but I lived hundreds of miles away and was only able to visit in holiday times. To make up to him I decided that I would write a letter to Dad each week. I would send it second class on Monday morning, so that he always got it on Wednesday. The routine was important to him, as it had been all his life.

I wrote from my home, from camping trips, from journeys abroad — including Australia and Iceland — and even once from hospital. He never wrote back but he rang me when he could.

Fourteen years later, when Dad died, I discovered that he had kept all the letters I had sent him, dating from the early 1980s. They were stored in his bedside dresser. There were around 700 altogether.

These letters stimulated me to write my fictional story about how Vi manages her new job as a Headteacher in a village school and how her father copes with loss.

This is a work inspired by my father, all other characters are fictitious and all the places are imaginary and created by me.

Chapter 1

An end and a beginning

September Sunday

Dear Dad,

I have good news at last. I have just got a letter asking me to go for an interview. Can you believe it? It's for a Headteacher at a little village school. The village is called Fish – a funny name don't you think? It is a lovely little place right out in the middle of nowhere, I reckon it will take me about forty minutes to get there. But I'm getting ahead of myself – I haven't got the job yet! Questions they might ask, keep on coming into my head. I have so many ideas and I am sure I can make a good job of it, if only they will give me a chance.

I am off shopping tomorrow, after school, to get some new clothes, I need to create a good impression. You always say that first impression counts, and the clothes that I am wearing, for school now, will not count for much.

I have studied the Headmistress, where I work, and have taken notice of what she is wearing. I will copy her, even down to her big handbag. Mam always looked smart, and I will try to think of her outfits when I choose mine. I want to think that she would be proud of me.

I hope that things are growing well in your garden.

Love Vi xx

I am sitting outside the interview room, in County Hall, wearing my new navy suit from Marks and Spencer's with a big empty handbag at my side. It looks good and I feel smart. My heels are higher than I normally wear but they make me look taller. There will be another interview at Fish school later in the day.

"Miss Heron, come this way please." Mr Hall, one of the Primary School advisers, has popped his head round the second door in the long, echoing passageway. I stand up rather quickly, too quickly as it turns out, and my high heels slip on the highly polished parquet flooring. My feet splay out sideways and I take a few moments to regain composure.

I am suddenly aware of feeling very self-conscious in my new interview clothes. This unfamiliar outfit suddenly seems to belong to someone else. My clothes seem too big for me. Surely, I cannot have shrunk in just a few days?

We are sitting in a large modern room. Mr Hall, with his immaculate grey suit and his piercing dark eyes, begins to question me. I am extremely nervous and keep licking my lips. I want this job.

Then, out of the blue, I realise that I have lost my handbag, the new shiny one I bought to create a good impression. Where is it? I lose concentration and have to ask Mr Hall to repeat one of his questions. My voice comes out high pitched and I have a feeling of despair but then—

"Can you describe your classroom to me?"

Can I? Of course, I can!

It all tumbles out, the triumphs and the topics we have been working on together, the children and me. Mr Hall leans back listening, with his hands clasped behind his head.

The interview is over, and I am flushed and elated. Then, as I reach the foyer where I waited for interview, to complete my feeling of well-being, I see my handbag on the floor. It is near the chair where I must have left it all those ages ago.

The second interview at the school will be more difficult. The thought of my name does not help either. I have always been proud of my surname 'Heron', it is different and there are not many around. It sticks in people's minds, and they tend to remember me. But now I am not so sure, will it sound silly in connection with a village called Fish? After all a heron eats fish.

I chug into the school drive and park my car carefully. I always think that parking neatly makes my old, battered car, at the very least, look cared for. I grab my handbag and walk up the steps carefully.

"The interviews are taking place in the vicarage down the road."

I look up to see where this cultured voice is coming from. There, at the top of the steps, stands a woman wearing expensive looking co-ordinating clothes, even her scarf matches. Her blonde hair, so carefully set, has not a strand out of place. I feel positively underdressed in my M&S suit compared to her.

"Have I made a mistake or something?" I stammer.

"Change of plans, Mr Norman could not accommodate the interviews," she replies confidently, as if all this is a normal event for her. 'Bad organisation,' I think, 'why weren't we told before?'.

The old vicarage is surrounded by swaying trees, so tall that they seem to engulf the building. An old lady answers the doorbell and shows me to a room on the left. A huge barking black dog comes bounding up. The old lady drags him by the collar just as he is about to go up my skirt (is my hemline too high?). The door slams and I am on my own in a room full of flowery armchairs. My nerves get the better of me again and I wonder if there is a chair for every candidate.

A motor bike roars up and it is not long before the rider is shown into the room with barking dog and strong old lady.

The man is dressed in leathers complete with helmet and goggles. He slowly reveals himself and it turns out that he is a good-looking young man called Mr Lewis. He teaches in a village school nearby. He is bound to be better than me.

"I hoped to create a good impression," he tells me breathlessly. "I intended to arrive early and get all this gear off before anyone else arrived, but I took the wrong turning and, when I finally arrived at the school, I was told to come here."

3

Thank goodness, he is nervous too. I am beginning to like him, and we are just starting a conversation about what they are likely to ask, when he is called out of the room.

I am on my own again and this fussy rose room is beginning to get on my nerves. I look at some wedding photos and an old gilt framed picture of a dog. I cannot stay any longer. I gently take hold of the white doorknob and turn. I peep out into the corridor, there is no one there and more importantly the dog does not seem to be lurking. I sneak into the hall, and I feel better already. There seems to be more air here.

Then I hear voices in the interview room opposite. I should not be listening. I creep back to my flowery cell and sit down, staring at the door.

Eventually, an Education Officer, I vaguely remember floating around County Hall, shows me into the room.

I blink to adjust to the darkness. Black oak panels stretch from floor to ceiling. The one gigantic window somehow does not seem to alleviate the situation, perhaps it is all the struggling undergrowth outside. Eight faces peer at me over the top of the mahogany dining room table. They can only just fit round and when I sit down in the vacant chair, they are all too close for comfort.

I am introduced to everyone but as soon as the introductions finish, I have forgotten all their names.

"It's such a shame the Lord is not here," sighs the little old lady in the corner. The vicar nods. What on earth are they talking about? The Lord? Surely, they are not serious? But no one looks surprised.

"I'll fire first, Miss Heron, and then we will go anticlockwise round the table," the old man fires.

"Forgive my asking, Miss Heron, but how are you, as a woman, going to teach football?" I briefly wonder if they ask men if they can teach netball, but it is not for me to do the wondering.

"Oh, I quite enjoy football. In my present school, I have been taking football practice at lunchtime for several years."

"Speak up, my dear, I am a trifle deaf."

"It won't be a problem," I shout. The old man sits back and says no more.

The rest of the questions are standard, as are my answers, it all sounds so general and any one of the candidates would answer the same as me.

The big red-faced vicar is getting ready for his question now. He runs his hands through his thin grey hair and asks, "Now be honest, Miss Heron, do you think that vicars can be a help when they come into school?" Well, what can I say? I mumble something about him being welcome, I go carefully as I know I am on thin ice here.

"Thank you, Miss Heron, all the other questions that I had prepared have already been asked by the good people on my left and so I have nothing further to add to the proceedings, at this moment in time." The vicar leans back, and I can see that he seems even more red in the face than before.

I am now looking at a very resolute looking man who is from County Hall. He has been taking copious notes all the time. He begins to grill me, but I can see a twinkle in his eyes and that makes me feel good.

What can I offer a country school? How would I organise the curriculum? Are country schools better or worse than town schools and why? I love all this; it is what I have been waiting for. I can hardly stop talking. I am full of ideas which come tumbling out. The Education Officer asks similar questions, and he leans forward with his hands clasped while I answer, unable to contain my enthusiasm for teaching. I sit back at last, flushed, and excited. As a final thought, I share some photos of my present classroom and children's work, from my new handbag which came in useful after all.

I look at the faces of the people who hold my future and the future of Fish village school in their hands. They look tired.

As I leave, I hear the old deaf man say, "Funny her name being 'Heron', when she's applying to Fish school, don't you think?"

I see Mr Lewis standing on the outside doorstep, as I leave the interviewing room, I join him. We look at the gigantic ash trees already losing their leaves. There is one more candidate being interviewed, he is a Deputy Head.

Mr Lewis and I go for a walk, and he solves a mystery for me. He knows who 'the Lord' is, they were referring to Lord Shawell who lived in Fish for many years and died only recently at the age of ninety. Many of the villagers came to rely on him and he made a good deal of the decisions regarding the village.

Eventually, we return to our little flower room. We are joined by the last candidate who is older and more experienced than us two. We wait in silence. I stare at the flower strewn carpet and dare not even look up as the Education Officer breezes into the room.

"After careful consideration, the committee has decided to appoint Miss Heron." He seems to have taken ages to deliver his speech, as if in slow motion, while the two men candidates get up and shake my hand.

I return to the dark interview room where tea is being served. There is a flowery tea service with matching teapot. The vicar is 'mother' and is pouring for everyone. A huge sponge cake is sliced by the old lady, and everyone tucks in. No one notices me, at first.

"That young one – well he only looked about eighteen years old – it's like policemen they seem to be getting younger and younger."

"What did you say? Are you talking about that old one that applied? He can't have many years left…"

They break off their conversations when they finally notice me.

"Welcome aboard," says the vicar, and he invites me to 'partake'.

After a decent interval of time, I make my excuses and leave. I get back into my battered old car and drive away as fast as I can. I am suddenly full of doubts again and wonder if I can do this job after all.

As soon as I am home, the phone rings.

"Is that you?"

"Hello, Dad. How are you?"

"Oh, you know."

"Not easy."

"No. How did you get on?"

"I got the job."

"That's what I wanted to hear. I've got the last lot of potatoes up. There'll be too many now there's just me, you know. It's a good crop this year. I'll talk to you later on in the week. But you got the job you say?"

"Yes!"

I decided to go back to Fish at night to have a good look. When I had been to the school before, I had been single minded in preparing for the interview. And being so intent I had not looked sideways.

It is a clear night and a big moon casts black shadows on the looming hills not far away; it makes them seem dark and somehow sinister. I take my torch from the car and peer in through the windows, working my way round the building.

Fish school is on the edge of the village. The church is just up the road, its dark outline towers over a few clustered houses. There is an eerie silence.

Strangely, for a country school, the building is fairly modern. I really wish now that it were an old building and almost in ruins, then no one would expect too much of me, what with the poor facilities.

I am getting scared, no, really scared, and wonder, for the umpteenth time, what I have let myself in for. I stare through the glass again but all I can see now is a circle from the torch and my big wide eyes. I walk around the building, there is my classroom with a side door from the outside leading to the class cloakroom. Then I turn the corner and see the Infant room with its own door. The next corner I turn has windows from the kitchen and stores with blinds drawn. The flat roofed hall is next and then I am back to the main door and staffroom which looks onto the car park.

I sit on the cold concrete steps. A mist is beginning to come down and the moon fades and finally disappears. I shiver and run to the car then head for home. I have two months' notice to work in my present school and there is a lot to organise before I take up post here.

October Sunday

Dear Dad,

How are you? Things are going well for my last term at Newford school, the children in my class in town are excited about our Harvest Festival service which will be on Monday. I sometimes tell them about our harvest on the farm and how we children all had to work. I tell them about the big steam engine and the pale orange threshing machine and how it separated the corn heads from the straw and chaff. I haven't told them about the rats that used to run out, with us children in hot pursuit carrying pitch forks! Harvest is far removed from farming here in town and a lot of the food they eat comes from tins.

I expect that you are digging your vegetable garden over getting it ready for the winter. What about your leeks, how are they doing? It's a good job that there is no garden here in this little rented house. I just haven't got the time for gardening now I am thinking of my new job.

I'm going to start looking for a new house tomorrow, I have decided that I need to live nearer Fish and time is getting on.

Love Vi xx

The next day I strike lucky, there is a house for sale in a large village called Wenbrook. Well, the locals call it a village, but

8

it has grown and has two housing estates now and some shops. It is in a nice area, though, and is surrounded by hills not too far from Fish.

This house has been on the market for some time, and I can tell why when I go inside. It smells; it's the purple carpet. You could not live with that for long, who would buy a stinky house? I did! I made an offer, and the deal was done. It is not as if I have time to look around or be too picky. I ring Dad.

"Hello, Dad, how are you?"

"Oh, you know."

"Yes, it's hard going."

"Aye, but why have you rung?"

"I've just bought a house."

"That's fast."

"Yes, well it was too good to miss. I have a bit of a deposit and I have no house to sell."

"So, it should be a quick sale."

"I hope so, the owner is a farmer and he bought it for his daughter, but she was used to country life and didn't like living there."

"Did you bid him down?"

"Yes, by two thousand and we made a verbal agreement."

"He'll keep his side of the bargain if he's a farmer. A gentleman's word is his bond. He'll want to sell because he'll be losing money with the house if nobody is living there – it's dead money for a farmer."

Dad was right, the house sale did go through quickly and in no time at all I was arranging a mortgage and assuring the building society that I could afford to make my payments. Everything is happening so quickly.

At the end of term, I do a quick round to say goodbye to my neighbours. I do not know many of them very well, but Cathy has been closer and we have gone out together for a laugh and a chatter sometimes. I knock but there is no answer. I peep through the letter box and shout my goodbyes just in case she is there and is in the bath or something. I have not got time to wait, I am following the removal van.

As I leave, I look in my car rear mirror and see Cathy in a dressing gown standing on the pavement waving. I peep the horn then go around the corner and disappear on my way to Wenbrook village.

Chapter 2

Teething problems

It is the Christmas holidays at last. I am glad that the term has ended, and I have left my old job. It is not that I did not like it, but so far, I have had to do what my Headteacher says. She is old and not wanting to try any new ideas. I am sure she is just waiting to retire. But I cannot wait.

My headship does not begin until the new year and I am now in a sort of limbo. I am waiting to be the Head of Fish school, until then I have a short respite.

The new house, 10, Oak Rise, has a massive garden and I go out to have a proper look. I bought it in a hurry and did not really think about what the garden was like. I didn't even want a garden. It is overgrown and the lawn has not been cut for a long time. At the bottom of the long wide strip, I can see a jungle of shrubs and trees. Oh no! I should have checked the garden size before I bought the house, but it is too late now. I close the door to concentrate on the inside.

I have not got much furniture and I have scattered a few chairs around and put my precious house plants in very empty looking spaces. The lounge is long with picture windows at each end. They need big curtains and I have no spare money for these now. In fact, I have not any money, I am now paying a huge mortgage and I am saving for a new car.

I am beginning to wonder if this house is such a good buy after all. For one thing I do not know how to cope with the smelly carpet. I have vacuumed it quite a few times, but I am not sure I have made any difference. The purple smell sneaks out into the entrance hall and slithers upstairs onto the landing. No wonder they were keen to sell the house to me. And there is another thing. I cannot get the central heating to work. I bought some oil, so that is not the problem. I gingerly looked in the boiler cupboard to see if there were any switches to turn but I could not see any.

That evening I go next door, down the road, to ask for help. Bill is as amiable as he looks. He puts his slippers on and tucks his shirt into his trousers half-heartedly. His shirt tails hang behind and he gives up all attempts to control them. He trundles round to my house to investigate. He taps my oil tank. A hollow sound echoes round the metal container.

"It's empty," he says smiling then frowning.

"It can't be, I had oil delivered."

"It is. I reckon it is you know."

First the smell of the carpet, now a leaking oil tank. I thought I was so clever buying this house, and now I know I am not.

I get some torches and we decide to go hunting round the house for the missing precious oil. We look on the concrete and on the weedy garden, then we search in the overgrown grass. I wonder what I would do if I found it as it trickled along.

I start to laugh as Bill bends double, earnestly parting the long undergrowth, peering with his nose almost on the ground.

"You want to check your insurance policy," he says, we laugh together and then he trundles back to his house with his shirt tails showing up like sails in the dark night. When he has gone, I do not find things so funny, what is there to laugh about being in debt and not being comfortable?

I wake at about six in the morning, from my troubled sleep, to someone shouting below my window. It is Bill.

"There's a wheel." He shouts.

"What do you mean?" I shout back through the open window.

"Come down, I'll show you."

I rush down the stairs and without stopping to put a coat on, I dash outside to the oil tank where Bill is standing triumphant. His legs are astride, and he is pointing to the side where I can see a tiny wheel. He is not wearing a coat either.

"You turn this wheel look. Just next to the tank. I'd forgotten about it." He turns. I go inside and switch the heating on. Everything bursts into action. Bill pokes his head in through the door smiling and giving me a thumbs up sign. I grin back, I have wet feet and my nighty is crumpled, but I have heating. I get into bed again hearing the hum of the central heating below and the crack of the pipes and radiators as the reluctant hot water swirls around.

December Sunday

Dear Dad,

Everything has gone well here. I have settled into number ten and it feels like home. You would love the garden; it is big and there is a rich clay soil just right for vegetables and fruit. As soon as I have time, I will get going with digging the vegetable patch. There is an apple tree here, so that will be a treat for me in the autumn. There is a fishpond too and I am looking forward to clearing it out and stocking it with fish.

I bet your fish are still at the bottom of the pond – if your weather is like ours, they will stay there until spring.

We are getting some frosts, but I am snug and warm here in the house with modern oil central heating. I need to get some curtains for the lounge next year, until then I have closed that room off for the winter.

I am hoping to come to stay with you in a few days' time, when you ring I am sure that I will have sorted my plans.

See you soon, looking forward to being with you for Christmas.

Love Vi xx

I have invited Bill and Joyce round for supper this evening. I thought it would be nice to get to know them better especially as Bill was so kind about my 'lost oil'.

Bill's shirt is still hanging out.

"I'm so glad that it's all sorted; aren't you, Bill?" Bill does not reply, and Joyce gives him a nudge.

"Well, there was definitely a hollow sound, when I tapped your tank."

"Oh yes, I've been thinking about that. I know why it sounded empty. I only bought a quarter of a tank. You must have been tapping above the level."

"Why didn't you fill it?"

"Bill, that's none of your business." Joyce nudges him again.

They sit down and I get supper. They start arguing. It is about Joyce wanting Bill to get a new job so she can have more money to spend on the house.

"I always pay the bills, don't I? We've always got plenty of money to fill our tank, not like Vi."

Joyce changes the subject as she kicks Bill on the foot.

"Why did you want to be a headmistress, Vi?" Joyce smiles. "Weren't you happy just being a teacher?"

"Well, yes I have been happy, I love teaching, but I am looking for something more..."

"There you are, Bill," interrupts Joyce. "I'm going to look for something more, maybe I could get a job." No one answers. Bill pretends he has not heard and Joyce tugs at her skirt to try and hide a ladder in her tights. Bill pulls at his shirt collar twisting his red neck from side to side and dislodging his tie.

They shuffle off home, arm in arm, at about ten o'clock. I stand at the door and then turn indoors. But I cannot settle and start worrying about my oil again, and although I should know better, I go to the tank just to be sure. I bend double and then with my ear to the cold metal, I tap. Is that a hollow sound or is that a full sound? I tap on the lower part, and I tap on the upper half. Is there a difference? I just cannot help but worry and think that I ought to be able to run this house better if I am going to run a school.

"Looking for something, Headmistress?" Bill's voice makes me jump. I stand up and turn around to see him at his door laughing with a raised beer glass in his hand.

Lessons with Dad

Chapter 3

The first Christmas

I am going to see Cathy again. I have wrapped a Christmas mug for her as a present. It is a bit of a joke as it is printed, 'The man in your life', and on the back is a picture of Father Christmas. I know that it is not much, but we have a laugh. Neither of us has a man in our lives at the moment.

Cathy works in a local garden centre on the outskirts of town. She once tied herself to the oak tree in the middle of the field next to the centre. She tried to stop it being cut down for a housing estate. But it was no good, the police cut her free and the tree was removed. I admire her dedication and I hope that I can be as strong as she is about my beliefs in education.

"You should see my garden, Cathy, it's an absolute mess."

"Why don't I come and sort it sometime? I would love that."

"Well maybe, but not until I can afford to pay you. It wouldn't be fair." We have a meal; it is vegetarian and all cooked by Cathy from fresh ingredients. We chat and drink some organic wine. I relax with her. I like her. But I must be off; I have a lot to do.

When I get home, Dad rings, it is then that I suddenly realise that Mother will not be there this Christmas. Of course, I knew she would not be there. She died in the summer but sometimes, in my busy life, I forget and then with a jerk, the reality hits me and I stop to regain composure.

"Hello, is that you?"

"Hello, Dad – I will set off early, tomorrow."

"Aye, that's what I wanted to hear. What time will you get here?"

"It'll be about three in the afternoon, I should think."

"All being well."

"Yes, as long as there aren't any hold ups."

"I saw your mam last night."

"What?"

"I saw your mam last night."

"What do you mean, Dad?"

"She came into our bedroom. She said she would never leave me. I asked her not to leave me when she wasn't very well and she said, 'I won't ever leave you'."

"What did you do when you saw her?"

"I said 'Hello' and she said 'Hello' and then I fell asleep with her there."

I do not know what to say, I must not upset him, so I say nothing. In any case I have no time to think, I am hurrying about getting ready to go and see him.

I arrive late, Dad is looking out of the window staring. I wonder how long he has been there waiting for my old car to come down the drive. I settle into a routine of cooking, shopping, and cleaning, Dad does not seem to do much of either. He starts writing a few last-minute Christmas cards for relatives. I lean over and notice that he is writing both their names. But Mother is not here. She is dead. Her upright Windsor chair standing near the fire is empty and has been since the summer.

"Mam is not here, Dad."

"She would want me to put her name on the cards, like we always did, together. She said that she would never leave me."

We get through Christmas as best we can, following the familiar old established routine except, of course, there is too much time. This is the time when we used to help my mother with all she needed. The day was never long enough. Now the day is too long and there are big blank gaps, and her chair stands yawning and bare. It is in the same place as it always has been. Its blue cushion is always smooth and plumped up.

I cook a turkey and Dad sharpens his carving knife on a round file with a bone handle. I cook his sprouts and mash his potatoes. I make a gravy. It looks good and smells good, but we hardly touch it. We are not hungry, somehow.

I gave Dad a little rug for Christmas to put over his legs and feet when he has had his lunch. It is the time that he always rests. He always has. When he was working on his farm, he had his meal at twelve noon, prompt, then he rested until one o'clock. He always had a mug of tea before going out to work again. He has done it all his life and sees no reason to change.

He strokes the rug with his thumb as we watch the Queen's speech on the television. This has always been part of our routine, and we are pretending that everything is normal, when it is not.

"Your mam liked the Queen, you know."

"I know, she liked all the Royal Family. She liked the way they dressed and the Norman Hartnell style."

"She looked like the Queen; you know. Your mam had a look of her. Always smart and tidy."

We do not mention Mother again, except when we go to her grave in the churchyard at Gumbalding. We take a wreath and Dad gets on with tidying up the soil. He has brought a spade.

"It'll all settle. It takes a bit of time to bed down." He puts the finishing touches to it with his unflinching hands, patting and smoothing the familiar soil. This is the soil he has known all his life; the church stands in a field that he once farmed.

His big hands, with permanently black nails, unhesitatingly handle the clods and place them in order. It is as if he is covering her with the rug, that I gave him, just as if she is safely tucked up in bed.

He turns, saying suddenly, "Walk on." He used to say that to his horses and then to Mam when she was finding it hard to move. We quickly get back into my car.

It is hard to leave Dad, but I must hurry back to number ten and get ready for the new term. I pile everything into the car and Dad comes out with two big parcels. He packs them in between my case and bags. Then he squeezes in three blackcurrant bushes he has just dug up.

"They're just the thing for your garden, you'll be glad of them in the summer when you start picking." Soil spills out of the newspaper they are wrapped in, and their roots seem to have a life of their own, working under and around my luggage.

Dad does not wait to see me off, he hurries into his garden and stares intently at his fruit trees with his back to me. I start my car up and inch down the drive. We do not wave and do not look at each other.

Home at last, I stagger in with my bags and cases. The blackcurrant bushes are lolling sideways, like wild things, with their unruly roots and straight stems. Soil is everywhere. I put them outside, by the back door, ignoring the huge swathe of unkempt garden stretching into the dusk.

The parcels reveal two pairs of big velvet curtains. I remember them hanging in the farmhouse before my parents had to move to their bungalow because Mam was not well. They will be so good here. I will hang them tomorrow, ready for the new year. Now I can use the lounge at night, and I will be warm with no danger of neighbours staring in.

The old year is coming to an end and so has my day. I go to bed, but even though I am tired I do not sleep. Then, when I hear the church clock strike twelve, I realise that from now on I am officially the Head at Fish school.

I go down for breakfast and there on the door mat is a key. This will be the key to my school. 'My school', I pick it up and roll it in my hand. Mr Norman must have pushed it through my letter box. He had been the 'Acting Head' at the school, the last true Head resigned because of ill health. The Education Authority did not have time to appoint, so they put someone in 'to hold the reins' until a new Head could be chosen.

Mr Norman stayed for a year and then went back to being a senior teacher in a large school in town. I am surprised that he did not get a headship. Maybe he was not too good at Fish. Maybe I will be able to be good.

I look at the key again. An ordinary looking key, it is small and says 'Master' on it. I bristle at the implication, but I know that it could not say 'Mistress'. I also know, of course, that now I am the person that can open all main doors to the building.

This is the key to my future. Despite my misgivings about the writing on it, I feel inspired.

The journey to school is beautiful. There are open fields on either side of the road, followed by a wooded stretch. The sun is behind me, and it lights up the trees, crisp and bare, this winter morning. A heron flies over the road in front of me and its white wings catch the light. The calm beats take it on its way.

I arrive to be greeted by absolute silence surrounding the school. I am so excited that I am sure my hammering heart will break the peace. I hold the key and put it gingerly into the lock. I turn it with a trembling hand. Nothing happens. I try again. Nothing. Finally, I push my whole body against the door and turn with force. It opens suddenly, and I am catapulted into the front entrance.

The school is freezing. It is colder in here than outside. I walk into the hall on the left and see that Mr Norman has not cleared up after Christmas. From every ceiling tile is suspended the most beautiful shiny picture, each one depicting an aspect of the Nativity. I can almost smell the Christmas dinner and see the children playing games in their best clothes. I can hear their laughter. But my mood soon changes.

I suddenly shiver, not only from the cold, but from the realisation that I am the one that must deal with these flouncing sparklers. They seem so inappropriate now as they defiantly jingle and jeer at me from their high swings. They are far too high for me to reach and they are in the middle of the room.

I drag the big PE frame into the hall and begin my grim and difficult task of dismantling the Christmas 'jesters'. When I have finished, I sit exhausted on the hall floor. I stare up to the high ceiling and see bits of limp string hanging there, while the grotesque crumpled figures lie twisted on the floor.

Now for my office, which doubles as the staffroom, my desk is there along with one for the ancillary helper, Mrs Plane. I open my top desk drawer and there I find a jumble of clips, drawing pins, rubber bands, unsharpened pencils and felt tips without tops. I tip the whole drawer full into the bin, throwing caution to the wind. It is not like me, but I have wasted so much time with the decorations and I must get on.

On the top of my desk there is a whole mass of papers including two wrapped Christmas presents and an ashtray with a half cigarette in it. Do you know, it looks as if Mr Norman has been interrupted in the middle of his work. It is as if he has just popped out and will be back again at any moment. It really does seem as if I am sitting in Mr Norman's very own lounge chair going through his personal belongings. But there is no sign of him and, of course, he will not be back.

I am afraid I throw most of the papers in the bin, which is now overflowing. I have no idea what most of the documents are about.

In the rest of the desk drawers, I find lots more personal things belonging to Mr Norman. The children seemed to have liked him. There is a pile of Good Luck cards from them to him, a tie pin, several little boxed ornaments, and a fountain pen. I collect all these in a bag ready to take them to his school as soon as possible.

There, that is finished, now I look round at the walls, they are covered in pin boards and every little space is plastered with letters, notices, and instructions. The older papers are curling round and almost meet in the middle. I work methodically round the room. Daringly, I decided to throw any letters and documents away if they are over three years old. It is a gamble as I have not much idea of what is important and what is not, but the whole place is chocked with paper, and I must do something to clear a way through.

I am at a loss really. What, for instance, do I do about the huge, illustrated poster on mouth-to-mouth resuscitation? I bin it and continually add to Mr Norman's personal bag.

Now, I am ready to look inside the big, fitted cupboard. What is in here? I open the door and charts come rolling out and zigzag at my feet. Then a guillotine, which was precariously balanced on a shelf, falls and the blade snaps at my toes. The shelves are crammed with everything imaginable. I find perfume, hairspray, empty tubes of glue, wallpaper, and egg boxes, it is difficult to remotely connect many of the objects with education. Does anyone ever use this stuff?

What can I do? It will take hours to sort, and I have not the time just now. I need to be thinking about the children's education. I carefully close the doors. I do not want to upset the applecart, so to speak, and I tiptoe away. When I get to my desk, I go back and take the precaution of propping a chair against the door of the cupboards.

How could Mr Norman have left such a mess? I am fed up with him and I decided there and then that I am not going to be bothered with any of his personal belongings and I tip them all into the bin. That will serve him right.

The front door bangs and I jump, but before I can move, Mrs Dunn, the school cleaner, bustles in.

"My, you've made a mess!" She disapproves of the piles of rubbish and takes a sharp breath in. Her chest puffs out. She rushes at the scraps of paper on the floor with a big black plastic bag in her hand. I feel sorry that she must do this and try to help her, she looks thin and old. However, I am all fingers and thumbs, and she does the job quickly and deftly, leaving me standing impotently with a few limp scraps of paper. She hurries off in a flurry with another quick intake of breath.

But when I go into the hall, I see Mrs Dunn standing with my office bin in one hand and with the other she is carefully fishing out Mr Norman's belongings. One by one she sets them down on the table in front of her, reverently stroking each one. I move closer and I hear her sharp intake of breath again.

"Mrs Dunn, what are you doing? I have thrown those in the bin."

"I think Mr Norman will want these," she says. "What would the poor little kiddies think if they knew their gifts to him had been thrown away by you?" She gets out her duster and begins to clean each object carefully.

'What would the children think if they knew Mr Norman had not even bothered to take the gifts they gave him and that he hadn't even bothered to open some of them? Have you thought of that, Mrs Dunn?' I do not say anything, of course.

When I get home, I see Joyce opening her door beckoning me.

"Come in, come in, you look as if you could do with a cup of tea, I've just made one." I think of my house and the fire to be lit and the central heating not yet turned on. She ushers me into her warm, friendly lounge. It is decorated with extravagant flowered wallpaper and all her upholstery and cushions shout out with exuberance of colour. They do not match, there is no colour scheme but they all frolic alongside side by welcoming side.

I go home after a relaxing warming time with Joyce. I try not to think about Dad's blackcurrant bushes frosting at the back door, so carefully chosen by him, and so quickly stuffed into a quick shallow hole by me. They are really the last thing I want at this time. I cannot imagine going out and picking blackcurrants, what would I do with them? Pie making and jam making are so far from my busy schedule. But I do not want to let Dad down.

January Sunday

Dear Dad,

All is going well at school. I went in today and met the cleaner. She is very conscientious and keeps the school spick and span. It is a wonderful school and such a marvellous opportunity for me, I have so many ideas on how to teach and how to give these country children a real chance in life. I am very lucky.

24

Joyce, next door, is very friendly and gave me a cup of tea when I got home.

The blackcurrant bushes you gave me are safely planted; I am looking forward to having a pie from them in the summer.

Are your snowdrops showing yet? They always do so well in your soil; I hope that I have some too but so far there is no sign. I have decided to leave the garden how it is, for now, and then I can see what comes up and make changes next year once I know what is there.

There has been a green woodpecker in the garden. It had a black moustache and a red head, it was wonderful to see it land on the fence, then fly over and take a sip of water from the pond where it had just thawed. It reminded me of Mr Bantam my headmaster at Ringham. I don't really know why. Perhaps it was the red beret he used to wear. Do you remember him?

I hope that you are getting lots of visitors to your bird table. When I get sorted, I would like to feed the birds, there seem to be so many dodging in and out of the bushes here.

Love Vi xx

I know it is not true about planting his blackcurrant bushes. They are still only heeled in, but I want my letters to cheer him up and not worry him, so I have decided that there is no harm in a few 'white lies' in my letters.

Chapter 4

Mrs Plane drops in

The school greets me in as cold and foreign way today, just as it did yesterday. I go straight to the staffroom and sit at my desk. A pile of mail has arrived in big brown envelopes. I work through and deal with them as best I can. I have not been trained for this. I was trained as a teacher, and I think it is expected that I will just have picked up how to be a Headteacher. It is a quite different job and I wish that there was a handbook to tell me what to do, but there is not. There is no one to ask, there is only me and I am the one in charge.

To add to my feeling of helplessness, the filing cabinet is locked, and I have no key, so if there is any information in there, it is of no help to me now.

I remember reading a book once where a young man inherited a mill in the north of England, and he had not got a clue what to do. On the first day he just said, with a confidence he did not feel, "Get on with your work as usual, everyone." I wonder if it worked. Maybe I should adopt that 'wait and see what comes up policy', like I have done with my garden.

To make a positive move, I have arranged to meet Mrs Plane, the ancillary helper, today, so that we can get to know each other and discuss the office work together. I am looking forward to working with her. I did, of course, meet her when I came to look round the school, she was quiet and diligent and was getting on with her work without a fuss. I hope I do better with her than I did with Mrs Dunn, the cleaner.

I sit in my chair having a break and eating my sandwiches. I look around the staffroom. I am rather pleased with my efforts. The whole room is looking quite business-like and far more pleasant and organised. I have bought some plants and they look good in here making the room far more welcoming. Friendly but efficient, is the atmosphere I hope to create. I particularly like the white cyclamen on my desk. It really is the purest white and full of flowers.

I just begin to eat my apple when Mrs Plane makes her entrance. She is bang on time. 'Very good,' I think, this is a sign of respect and professionalism. I wonder what she will think of the room and all the changes I have made. I cannot wait to hear her comments. However, to my dismay, she does not seem to notice anything, least of all me, as she sludges over to her seat.

"Hello, Mrs Plane," I try to sound cheerful. "I am very grateful that you could spare the time to come and have a chat today." She gives me a very slight watery smile but does not say anything. Then she sits, looking at me, motionless with her hands carefully resting on her lap and her shoulders slightly hunched. Her Arran cardigan droops to her knees weighed down by huge buttons.

"What do you think of my new arrangements in the staffroom, Mrs Plane?" I just cannot resist asking, keeping my voice deliberately cheerful even though I am not getting any encouragement.

A few seconds tick slowly by. I wonder if she is shy or embarrassed, as she sits with her hands unmoving in her lap. I begin to feel uncomfortable, then suddenly she speaks.

"Oh, I've seen this room arranged in every possible way. Old Mr Jackson had the room like this ten years ago. It's just a fad, everything comes back if you wait long enough. The work has to be done just the same, and it always has been done however the desks are arranged."

I am disappointed and do not know how to reply, so I carry on eating my apple in silence. Then I suddenly feel foolish eating in front of her and hearing my 'crunch, crunch' echoing round the room.

I throw the core in the green metal bin.

"Well, let's get to work then." I sit up straight and try to sound business-like, casual conversation did not work. I launch straight in.

"Do you know where the filing cabinet key is? I don't seem to be able to find it and I would like..." I look at Mrs Plane and she is still sitting perfectly and is staring steadily at me. I stammer and for some reason my words do not come. Then I watch as she silently fishes into her handbag and produces a key, which she holds out to me. We eyeball each other in silence. I suppose it is the filing cabinet key, but I am not sure whether she intends me to take it. I do nothing.

"Mr Norman likes me to keep the cabinet locked and he likes me to keep the key for him." She whispers so quietly that I have to lean forwards to hear what she is saying. She makes it sound as if Mr Blinking Norman is coming back any minute to carry on where he left off. I am fed up with this.

"Well, I would like to keep the key from now on. I may want it when you're not here." I hope I sound confident, but I feel jumpy when I reach out for the key, and I snatch it from her. I can imagine she will close her hand at the last minute and we will have a tug of war. But she does not protest and does not shift her gaze.

I am in the middle of going through the forms to be dealt with and she is putting them one by one into her desk tray, when we hear a car swerve into the car park. I hear a screech of brakes and then the slam of a car door. A man rushes in and flashes a smile at Mrs Plane before his piercing blue eyes turn to me. He holds his hand out.

"Hi, I'm James, Chair of the Parent Teachers' Association."

I get up and we walk into my classroom. I welcome the chance to stretch my legs.

"I see that you have met our Mrs Plane, how are you getting on with her?" He lights a cigarette and then carries on speaking, without waiting for a reply. "She works very hard for the school and knows all there is to know about the families here."

"She seems very quiet," I venture.

"I suppose it's easier for me, being a man." He smiles and takes another drag on his cigarette. It is then I hear something hit the window. We look out to see a rather large boy throwing stones.

"Miss 'eron, Miss 'eron."

"Do you know who that is?"

"Oh, it's only big Darren. He left the school at the end of the summer term to go to the Comprehensive in Newford. You'll meet his brother Neville soon, he's in your class."

"I'm not looking forward to that."

"Well I must be off. I'll send Darren on his way, he's harmless enough. Keep up the good work. See you soon." He flashes me his lovely smile and clicks his heels together, then giving me a mock salute, he dashes away. The front door bangs and he is gone.

Mrs Plane is waiting patiently with her hands on her lap.

She replies concisely to all my questions about the registers and dinner money but when I ask her how to use the office duplicator she says,

"I will do anything you need doing when I am here. It is temperamental, and you need to know what you are doing if you are going to touch it."

"Oh, don't worry, Mrs Plane, I am quite good with office equipment," I answer. She is looking out of the window.

"Well, thank you, Mrs Plane, that is all for the moment, though once the school is up and running, I am sure that there will be a lot of things we will need to discuss. Thank you for coming in."

I thought that she would get up now, but she does not move and is still looking out of the window. I feel awkward and so I get up and go to the loo. I lock myself in and wait until I hear her car moving away and then I feel safe to come out.

I decide to use my newly acquired key to open the filing cabinet. I slide the heavy top drawer out and it reveals a jumble of pamphlets, old papers and plant pots. The bottom drawer is full of old margarine tubs and a bottle of whisky. The other two drawers hold the files, but sorting is easy as I apply my three-year-old rule.

I sit in my chair tired but pleased with myself. It is then that I remember the whisky. I have not drunk whisky before. Cathy and I sometimes had a glass of her organic wine unless we were drinking mint tea. I pour myself half a cupful, it tastes sharp and stings my mouth, but a warm glow comes over me as it slips down my throat. I savour the moment and pour another half cup. Then as I put the bottle back, I see a rolled-up poster squashed under the margarine tubs. I tug it out.

'*Colorado beetle warning. Have you seen this pest? Take action immediately – call the police.*'

Mrs Dunn, turns up unexpectedly with a damp cloth and starts to wipe bits of my apple, slowly turning brown, from the sides of the bin. She takes a sharp breath in.

It is so cold now that it seems even my cyclamen has lost the will to live. Its white flowers have flopped over, flaccid on the pot. Mrs Dunn rushes out, black poly rubbish bag rustling as she goes. I hear a noise outside.

"Miss 'eron."

Have you seen this pest?

"Miss 'eron."

Take action immediately.

Surely it can't be him?

After identification.

It is Darren again.

Phone the police.

He walks straight into the staffroom.

"Miss 'eron, I've brought you this plant."

False alarm, it was the whisky talking.

He carefully lifts out an old geranium from a crumpled paper bag.

"Mum was throwing it out, she was fed up with it, so I brought it for you." Maybe it is the whisky but for some reason I find it hard to be angry with this boy. He looks so sad with his head bowed holding the dirty plant pot. He puts it on my desk and the bright red petals fall from the only flower.

"It don't like being moved."

"I don't think many of us do, Darren." He laughs but I do not imagine he knows what I mean.

For some reason Dad's blackcurrant bushes spring into my mind again. I have not put them out yet, they are still heeled in at the back door. I just haven't had the time. I am not sure that I will have time to pick when the fruit comes. But I cannot let Dad down; I must plant them properly and soon. For now, I must get on with clearing up, so that I am ready for the pupils.

January Sunday

Dear Dad,

I hope it is not too cold for you. We have been freezing here but getting a bit milder. Mind you we shouldn't grumble as we are still in winter and we have been quite lucky so far.

I went into school again on Friday and met the ancillary helper who works in the office for me. She is very capable and a no-nonsense type of person and will be a great help to me in my job.

I also met one of the lads who used to come to the school, he is big and strong and helped me with clearing lots of old papers away. He was a real help to Mrs Dunn, our cleaner, as well.

I found a huge glossy Colorado beetle poster in school. There was a picture of a big stripy creature, it looked very fearsome, but I don't suppose we get any round here. I thought they attacked potatoes and I didn't think that they were in this country. My friend Cathy says that the last one found here was five years ago in the UK.

Anyway, I have far more things to think about, as you can imagine. But it is a government poster, so I didn't like to throw it out. I took it to the kitchen, for the cook to look at, in case the beetle comes in on the potatoes.

How are your leeks doing? I bet you are eating them now – they looked good and strong when I was with you at Christmas. Maybe when I come at half-term, we can make some leek soup. I am looking forward to that already.

My garden is full of plants and I can't wait to see what comes up in the spring. I think I will get those fish for the fishpond when the weather warms a bit and then we can compare notes.

Off to bed now

Love Vi xx

Chapter 5

Miss Faye floats by

Rushing on my way to school this cold morning I see that heron again. At least, I assume it is the same one, but I suppose one heron looks much the same as another. It calmly flies over the road as if it has not a care in the world. It flaps down low over the road with its chest sticking out and then gains height to land in a nearby willow tree. I would love to stop the car and just marvel at this creature for a while, but I must hurry and I press the accelerator and speed on my way. The bird lifts my spirits, it seems to have become my good luck symbol.

I decide to tackle my classroom this morning before the infant teacher, Miss Sara Faye, arrives for our first staff meeting. She is young and in her third year of teaching. I am looking forward to discussing education with her. Young people are usually full of enthusiasm and ideas, trying to do what people my age think impossible.

Mr Norman has left my classroom much as he left the hall with the decorations. It is as if he just abandoned everything at the end of term, without a backward glance at what he was leaving behind. A bench down the middle of my room is littered with what looks like old junk from a garage. The modern County Advisers, who are really inspectors, seem to like this sort of thing, it is called learning from the environment. And the children must have first-hand experience. I cannot really see the purpose of this display, but I am sure Mr Norman had his reasons.

I start to sort my classroom and I am so absorbed that I lose track of time, and before I know it two o'clock has arrived. Goodness! I promised to meet Miss Faye at two! I rush off to the staffroom and eat my sandwiches and gulp coffee from my flask.

Miss Faye arrives at 2.30pm in a flurry of drifting material and perfume. She really is a wide-eyed beauty, and her voice is soft and gentle.

"I am so sorry I am late, Vi. I had to get a lift here with my friend and she had no petrol in her car, so we had to push it to the garage. You see, I've only just found out that the tax disc on my car is out of date." Her gentle voice caresses my ears. I try, and fail, to imagine this willow of a person pushing a car in her high heels and floating material. She trips off to her classroom carrying a box of bark and driftwood.

"I'll just take these, then I'll make us both a nice cup of coffee."

"That would be lovely," I say, even though I have just had a coffee. I want to appear to be friendly.

Off she goes to the kitchen and comes back with a tray, complete with cloth, biscuits, and school green cups. She passes me a cup of coffee and a biscuit plate.

"What topic are you working on this term?" I spoil the cosy atmosphere a bit abruptly. But this is a staff meeting after all.

"Oh, something to do with the environment, I think. Perhaps I can take the children for some walks in Fish woods and look around. It's so beautiful there, you know. I can teach them about wildflowers."

"Wildflowers?" I am beginning to panic, after all it is winter.

"Yes, the little children love flowers, you know."

She makes it all sound so attractive. I am sure that the children will enjoy themselves and I am lulled by her gentle voice as she extols the virtues of the countryside. But then warning bells ring in my head as I remind myself again that it is winter. What are the children going to learn? What is her aim?

I must move this meeting on.

"Well, Sara, I can see that you have given this some thought, but I would like you to spend some more time and develop your ideas further. When you have decided on the work the children are going to do, we can meet up again later." I then suggest some ideas for development.

"Oh, that's a good idea," she says. She looks at me with her big eyes and long black lashes and she smiles gently. I suddenly feel old and drab next to her, she has obviously taken great care with her clothes today.

She certainly is not as absent minded about fashion as she is about her car tax. She is wearing a little purple chiffon scarf, a light silky blouse, and a fitted blue woollen skirt. Her tights match her scarf, and her peep-toe slingback shoes are a mixture of purple and navy straps. Perhaps I will be able to learn a few fashion tips from her.

I drag my mind back to our staff meeting. I tell Sara about the new maths scheme I have ordered.

"That's another good idea, maths isn't my strong point." She passes me another biscuit and I notice her mauve eye shadow.

"Is there anything you would like to ask me, Sara?" She smiles and makes a little shrug.

"Well, is there anything you are short of and would like me to get you, to help with your teaching?" Maybe she will highlight some equipment or books she has always wanted.

"I would really love some bean bags; you know those squashy floor cushions. They would be lovely for the children at story-time." She speaks gently and persuasively looking straight at me with those pool-like eyes of hers.

Squashy cushions are not exactly what I had in mind to develop our teaching, but I smile back.

"I must go and polish the leaves of the plants in my room," Sara sighs and gets up. "I have got some special spray which is supposed to do a good job." She trots off and then pops her head back through the door. "Oh sorry, you had finished the meeting, hadn't you?"

I suppose I had.

A man walks in, it is Mr Lewis from the interview. We laugh a bit nervously as we both remember the tension of the day.

"I thought they'd appoint you."

"I thought they'd appoint you."

"Anyway, I was pleased that you got it. I'd already had my luck for that week."

"What do you mean?"

"Well, when I came to look round the school, before the interview, I met Sara and we fell for each other straight away. I couldn't really concentrate on the interview, I felt that I had already found all I wanted in life."

I hear the front door bang and I look out of the window. I see James dash to his car and shoot off.

Suddenly, a red-faced Sara appears, Mr Lewis rushes to her and puts his arm round her trim waist.

"Sara, thank goodness you are here. Are you alright? I saw your car still in your drive. I knocked but no one was there." There is an edge of anxiety in his voice.

"Oh, Tim, it's lovely to see you." She buries her head in his stripy jumper and he strokes her hair.

"Vi, sorry, I didn't introduce you, this is Tim my new boyfriend, he teaches in the school in the next village, Bridlypool. Oh, I'd forgotten you met at the interview, silly me."

"We must be off – got a party tonight. Byee." I watch as they zoom off on Tim's motorbike, Sara's hair is streaming in the wind. Shouldn't she be wearing a crash helmet?

I survey the tray of dirty pots and smell a lingering drift of heather perfume. A sadness comes over me, but it is time for action.

Then, just before I get on with yet more clearing up, I open the bottom drawer in the filing cabinet and pour another drop of whisky into my coffee cup.

Cheers, Mr Norman!

January Sunday

Dear Dad,

We are having some very cold weather here I hope that you are managing to keep warm with that new rug I bought you.

Are you getting out in the garden? Mine is frozen solid so there is not a chance of doing any digging – at least I hope it will kill the weeds. I expect that you will have some Brussels sprouts still left and your leeks will still be going strong.

I have just had a meeting with my infant teacher. She is a lovely person; we had a little chat about education, and I think that we will get along very well. Mam would have loved her clothes; they were co-ordinated and made of beautiful floating material.

My classroom is the first one off the corridor, it is big and modern with lots of glass which makes it airy and light. It is fitted out with cupboards which have curtains instead of doors. I look out over trees and rolling countryside. It will be even more beautiful in the spring when the green buds burst with leaves.

The children don't have desks like you had when you were at school. They sit at tables and all their equipment and books are kept in grey trays which fit into units at the side of the room. I have been tidying up a bit and getting ready for the pupils.

I am looking forward to term starting so that I can meet the children. I have such a lot of ideas to help them with learning, I just can't wait to put them into practice.

I bet your bird table is full of birds. I saw a bag of nuts for sale, in a shop here in Wenbrook, yesterday. They were peanuts in a red netting bag. I bought them and hung them on a nail sticking out of my fence. I could hardly believe it when I opened the curtains this morning because a different woodpecker was on it, pecking away. This one was black and white, not green like the other one. It had a red rump. I wonder if you have seen one.

Thank you very much for the curtains. They fit my windows after I had pulled a bit at the threads on the tape, your windows must have been bigger than mine. They look so good and remind me of our farmhouse. They will keep my room warm as well.

Love Vi xx

Chapter 6

First day

I am getting ready for bed and the phone rings.

"Hello, is that you?"

"Hello, Dad. How are you?"

"Oh, you know. I've been thinking and I've had a good idea."

"What's that?"

"Well, you know how much I miss your mam. We have been married for nearly fifty years and I miss her even more when I am in bed."

"Yes, you must do." I am wondering where this is leading.

"Well, I've put our big bolster on her side of the bed."

"How does that help?"

"When I wake up in the night and put my arm out onto her side there isn't a big gap now. I feel the bolster and think that it is her. Then I go back to sleep."

"That's a good idea, Dad."

"Aye, I think it is. When do you start back at school?"

"Tomorrow."

"Let me know how you get on. Ta-ra."

The big day has arrived at last. This is the day. I have only had a few hours' sleep, what with all the anticipation and arrangements. Just as I was drifting off, another good idea for a lesson would spring to mind.

I pay more attention to my dress this morning with memories of Miss Sara Faye's outfit floating in her fairy grotto classroom. She has shamed me into thinking that I must try harder with my appearance. I put on my best outfit, the one that I wore for interview and then I rummage in a drawer for a chiffon scarf. I put on my high heeled shoes. But when I look in my mirror, I decide that Sara's influence has not done me much good.

I think that some people can look attractive even if they turn up in jumble sale clothes, they can still look like someone out of a fashion magazine. Then there are some people who always look frayed at the edges, as if they dressed in a hurry, no matter how long they took to get ready. I am one of those frayed at the edges people and Miss Faye is one of the beautiful people, seemingly without much effort. But I am nothing if not a trier and, at least, I know I have made an effort this morning. And as my mother always said, 'Practice makes perfect'.

I hope that is true for my work at school. I want to change so much that has gone before. But whatever I think, the staff seem extremely comfortable with the way things were and I will only get their backs up if start disagreeing, out loud, with everything that they are doing.

I set off for my first day. I am early, which is what I want. There are no cars in the car park, which is good as I want to be able to greet all the staff and welcome them to my territory so to speak (not the other way around). However, Beth, the cook is here, she lives in the village, I suppose she has walked. I pop my head round the kitchen door, and she makes me a cup of tea. She is so jolly and round, the opposite of Mrs Dunn in every way, I feel that I have known her, as a friend, all my life. She cuts up some parsley and tells me about a Headmistress at a school in the north of the county who lost her job. In the middle of this story, I notice Mrs Plane has appeared quietly like a shadow in the corner.

"She was such a nice person."

"Obviously too nice, if you ask me," says Mrs Plane.

"They say that everyone liked her," continued Beth.

"Some liked her too much."

"Well. That's true, I suppose. You see, Miss Heron, she ran away with a local farmer. He was married but they were so much in love. It was real love, despite all the unkind comments.

Mrs Plane is more aware of the story than me. Her husband knows him better as they are both farmers."

"Well, it can't have been true love because she came back without him." Mrs Plane does not smile.

"Ah well," sighs Beth, "true love never did run smooth."

"So, she went back to her school?" I ask.

"Oh no," answers Mrs Plane, "their vicar wouldn't have her on the premises again – he said that it would not be right for her to be teaching children about good and evil when she had committed such an act of wantonness – and in his own parish – under his very eyes."

"I suppose she had to lose her job," Beth sighs, "after being immoral like that. But they say she was a good headmistress."

"What happened to the farmer?"

"Oh, his wife took him back. Well, she had to really, what with her relying on him to run the farm. And of course, she had to think of their children..."

I decide that I have not time to listen to the rest of the story and I rush off to do some work. Beth's friendly reception has lulled me into a false sense of security. I bustle out, it will soon be nine o'clock when I must somehow get the school rolling into action. Miss Faye has arrived and is standing in the hall surrounded by a crowd of children who follow her as she drifts off up the corridor to her classroom. Nine o'clock is here, the hour I have dreaded and looked forward to for so long.

Nothing dramatic happens. Mrs Plane is now sitting at a table in the corridor with a Quality Street tin in front of her. My class line up in front of her. She has two queues. She deals with the short one first, these are the free school meal children. Their parents are unemployed or on low incomes. No one seems to mind that they are singled out in this way.

"Can't we have just one queue please, Mrs Plane? I don't want to embarrass the children who get free school meals."

"Oh, they don't mind. The short queue shuffles forward to be marked with 'f' in the dinner register. The remaining pupils hand in their dinner money then come back to my room and sit down.

"I'm not paying!" The silence of the queue is broken. I am alarmed by one of the older boys shouting.

"What seems to be the trouble, Mrs Plane?" I rush over to ask.

"Neville has to pay for his dinners now, we have had a letter about it." I take Neville aside so Mrs Plane can get on with the rest of her collecting.

"Neville, you have to pay, this letter says so," I explain firmly but gently.

"But I never pay. I'm on free meals, right? I go in the little queue and go first." We leave it there, Neville slumps off to his table, hands in pockets and his head down muttering in his fury.

Finally, when the dinner money routine is over, I greet the children and introduce myself. I have just started to tell them a little about who I am, when Miss Faye comes in carrying an over full school green cup of coffee. It is spilling everywhere but her smile is lovely. I glance over to Mrs Plane, and she is drinking her coffee from a huge brown pottery mug. I wonder what Miss Faye drinks out of, a white china one sprinkled with spring flowers dancing round the rim? I must say I am not keen on cups of coffee when school has begun, but I do not say anything. I just wait until Miss Faye has gone, then I pour the drink away down the sink. I look up to see Mrs Plane staring at me through glazed eyes.

My pupils are noticeably quiet. I finish telling them about the classes I have taught and then I settle them to write about themselves. It serves two purposes. It will tell me about their abilities and a little about their lives. There are no records of children's achievements left by Mr Norman so, getting them to write is a good beginning.

Then, I talk to each child individually and get each one to read to me. It is so good to talk to them at last. Neville is first.

He is a bit scruffy; his hair is uncombed, and his clothes are creased, but he chats away easily.

"I got this book last term, right. Well, I tried to read it, but it was a bit boring, right. Mr Norman, you know Mr Norman, right? Well, 'e says I've got to keep reading it even though it's boring, right."

The book is *Peter Pan*, an unabridged version. I do not imagine for one moment that Neville is able to relate to a story involving nannies and children's nurseries. He is only on chapter two, and he started the book well before Christmas. He knows exactly how many pages he has read and how many more he must read, but he cannot tell me about the story so far.

"Well, there's this boy, right. Well, 'e's called Peter Pan and 'e can fly, well, I think somebody can fly because there's a picture here of a lad with wings, right."

I decide it is time for a change and show Neville some books about monsters that I have brought in. Neville gives a wide grin.

"Mr Norman, right, well 'e wouldn't let us change a book until we'd read it. 'ey, monsters, great!" He goes round the class showing them his new book.

"Look here's a monster, right, well 'e's got a job cleaning, right, and 'e 'as to wear a pinny. 'e looks a right wally!" Now he shows off a picture of a huge purple monster wearing a frilly pink apron.

After our break I want to get on with maths. The new maths scheme, that I ordered, has not arrived yet, so I have made work cards for the children. Neville gives them out. After a delicious lunch, the children go out to play. I seize the chance to draft a letter to the parents to introduce myself and to let them know how much I am looking forward to meeting them and working with them to further their children's education. I hope to sound friendly and professional. I have found one or two copies of Mr Norman's letters to the parents, they seem chummy and casual, not my style at all, but I cannot help envying his seemingly easy relationships. On impulse I sign off, 'Best wishes, Vi Heron, Headteacher'.

It starts to rain. I leave my letter introducing myself to the parents on Mrs Plane's desk ready for her to type and I go over to see the children, who are tumbling in through the door, with rain glistening on their anoraks.

The hall roof is leaking, and the water seems to be running along the roof tiles and into my classroom. Caroline, dressed neatly in a dark green outfit, which looks like a school uniform, fetches a bucket. I am surprised that she has done this as so far, she has been noticeably quiet and shy. Perhaps it was her job last year. I know the bucket must be there, we cannot have a wet slippery floor, but it seems so bad, a big black bucket, after all my efforts to make the room look smart.

I have planned to do drama this afternoon. Rebecca, a chubby girl with a round face, comes over, looking sad, her mouth turned down, as if she will cry any moment.

"I don't feel very well," she whispers, and she hangs her head to one side.

"Oh dear, poor you, Rebecca, just sit at the side and watch. Don't join in for the moment." Everyone else is raring to go and full of energy. We walk down the corridor and into the hall.

I am ready to begin, when two men arrive and come over to me, they have brought the cleaning order and want to know where to leave it. In my hurry to get on with the lesson I ask them to leave the delivery in the corridor. It soon becomes evident that I have made a mistake. The men tramp in and out heaving heavy cardboard boxes full of toilet rolls and large containers.

One toilet roll falls out and lolls across the corridor floor. All this is too much for Neville and he begins to find drama funny. I stand him at the side to calm down.

"Sign this, love," says one of the men, pushing a piece of paper into my hands. I sign and turn back to Neville.

"Rebecca isn't really bad, she just don't like acting, she always does this, right," he says, seemingly trying to take attention away from his own behaviour.

Beth comes out of the kitchen and is sorry to bother me, but would I like her to order milk for the staff tea and coffee, and who is going to pay?

"Mr Norman used to pay for it himself, which was very kind of him," she adds.

"Why don't we have a kitty where we can all contribute?" I ask, thinking on my feet.

"What a good idea, I'll set that up straight away and get the order organised."

At the end of the day Neville grabs his reading book and dashes off. I notice him with someone at the gate. It must be his mum; she is talking casually as she leans on the fence flicking her long, blonde-streaked hair out of her eyes. She takes another puff at her cigarette and watches calmly as Neville starts waving his arms about before he comes dashing back to me. He stands angrily with his hands on his hips, legs astride.

"You know my dad, right?" Before I have time to answer he carries on. "You'll never guess what 'e' as been and gone and done." He is furious, he is pacing the path and his hands clench in fists.

"What is it, Neville?" I am concerned, what can his dad have done?

"'e's only been and gone and got a job."

I am relieved but I do not understand. "But that's good, Neville."

"'e's been and gone and got a job and I can't 'ave free meals no more. 'e's daft. I'm going to kill 'im." He spits out his words and then charges off.

Finally, I retreat to the staffroom. Mrs Plane has already completed the letter I left for her to type and it is on my desk. She has duplicated fifty copies. I am pleased with this until I notice that she has altered my ending and has signed me off as

'Yours sincerely, Miss Heron (Headmistress)'. Ah well, my efforts at being friendly like Mr Norman failed this time.

I decide to deal with the cleaning order, and I help Mrs Dunn clear it all away until her cupboard is full. We leave the rest of the order in the staffroom, where black polythene bags, loo rolls and paper towels push against the cupboard. I think that this is a good thing as, at least, this is extra pressure on the doors. The likelihood of them bursting open and disgorging their contents is more remote.

I am ready to go but pop back to my classroom to check everything is in order. Mrs Dunn is there heaving the carpet back.

"They don't know what we have to put up with here," she spits her words out angrily, "this hall roof has always leaked ever since it was built." She draws in her breath and sticks out her chest in disapproval as she rushes to get the mop.

I go to the staffroom and phone County Hall, no one answers, they will have all gone home as it is after five. I leave a message about the leaking roof then bundle piles of marking into my car and drive off.

It is the end of my first day 'teaching' at Fish school.

The next day, I am ready and in my classroom for a nine o'clock start, prompt. I had a sleepless night worrying about the leaky roof, but no sooner have we begun lessons than a voice shouts from the corridor.

"Hello, luv." Two workmen appear at my open door.

"Where's the headmaster?" one of them asks.

"I'm Miss Heron, the Headteacher." I am looking at them disapprovingly, they are too loud and will disturb the children's work.

"Oh, there was a bloke here last time we came, has he got promotion them?" A grin spreads across his face.

"What can I do for you? I am teaching this class and they need my attention." I can see Neville from the corner of my eye, he is craning his neck and taking a keen interest in our visitors.

"We've just come to look at the roof." Off they go to inspect the roof and I pick up the threads of our maths. We can hear them clomping about on the hall roof. But this is good news; I can hardly believe that County Hall has reacted so quickly.

Then they are back.

"There's two big plastic panels missing from the hall, you haven't seen them, have you? They would be about ten foot by four."

They must be joking. Surely, there could not have been such large sheets so loosely attached to a school building. What if one had blown off and hurt a child? I eye my class; I should be teaching.

"What do you want us to do?"

"Well, I need the roof repaired, so I guess that you need to order some more panels."

"Righty ho, but you realise that it'll take quite a few weeks for them to come. You know what it's like."

"Will that stop the leak?"

"Oh no that's a different job. We've just come for the headmaster's call out." One of them winks at me and they both clomp off. But they have not left the premises because, as I rush back to my maths lesson, I see these two characters searching up and down the hedgerow. Eventually they walk off empty handed.

January Sunday

Dear Dad,

The frosts we are having here will do your sprouts good – you always say that they need a good frost to bring out the flavour but maybe you are not getting the same weather as us.

Things are going well at school and it is lovely now I have met the children. There is a boy called Neville and I can't help liking him, but he is not easy. He is very independent and has a mind of his own. He is a real character. Rebecca is another pupil who I am getting to know, she is quite shy and a little bit

49

overweight which is probably why she doesn't like drama and PE. I did not like games very much and I wasn't any good at hockey when I was at school.

Do you remember that when you were married the village hockey club made an arch of hockey sticks to walk through? Mam must have been very athletic and good at hockey. I don't think that I take after her.

Our roof at school leaks – the hall has a flat roof. I know that you have never been keen on flat roofs – it stands to reason they will leak you always told me. I have reported it to the County and so I am sure that workmen will be coming to repair it soon. I remember our farmhouse roof leaking and some plaster falling into our bedroom when I was a little girl. Even though it was an inclined roof you always said that it needed to be steeper. Thank goodness the classrooms here at school have sloping tiled roofs, unlike the hall.

The hall is a good big space for us all, we dine in there and the kitchen staff only need to roll up a blind and serve us all from a counter. We have PE lessons there and all the ropes and bars swing out from the sides. Of course, we also have our assemblies in there too, with the whole school. I must think of something to say to the children every day for our service and our ancillary helper plays the piano for our hymns on Mondays and Fridays. Sometimes I play the hymn and sometimes a little girl called Caroline does it.

I hope you are getting a lot of birds on your bird table. But I hope that you are not getting too many starlings. I have seen them crowding your table and eating all the food if they can. They don't give you much chance to see the other smaller birds.

Do you remember that we used to think that starlings carried foot and mouth disease? We used to have massive murmurings of starlings all over our fields. I remember you and Uncle Sid going out to shoot them and keep them off our land for fear of the disease. Gwendy and I used to go out and 'rescue' the birds that were not yet dead. We wrapped them up and put them in boxes and fed them on bread and milk. I expect that we *thought that we were being kind. I would have been about eleven, so the year would have been around 1956 which is when there was a big outbreak of the disease.*

I am still seeing a lot of the black and white woodpecker, but I don't get to see the birds very much now, as it's dark when I get home. I'll see them at the weekend. I'm thinking of getting a bird table like you.

Love Vi xx

Chapter 7

All is not lost

It is snowing when I get up this morning and, as I drive along the country lane, the flakes get bigger, and the snow is thicker. I am wishing that I had brought my wellingtons. I feel rather foolish when I realise that I have come in my high heeled slingback shoes. I drive at crawling pace. I have not had much experience of driving in snow and so all I can do is grit my teeth and curl my toes as I lean forwards to peer out of the screen. There are no cars in the school car park when I arrive.

No one is here. Then, Mrs Dunn suddenly appears, like a genie. She takes a sharp intake of breath when she sees my shoes. And, with a shovel in her hand, she bends down and tries to scrape a path in the snow just in front of me. She stays in a doubled-up position as she scrapes. Scrape, step, scrape, step. It is almost like she is unrolling the red carpet for me until we reach the front door. She is so bundled up in several coats and I am surprised that she can bend. She is wearing her usual short green wellies.

"Oh well done, thank you, Mrs Dunn." I only notice the pun after I have said it and it is too late. Mrs Dunn stands and arches her back and ties her check headscarf more tightly under her chin.

"No good thanking me, you want to wear a warm overcoat and stout shoes in weather like this – you'll regret it!" Mrs Dunn scolds me with a sharp intake of breath.

The children are starting to arrive in ones and twos and Mrs Dunn, seeing another way of being useful, dashes indoors and helps the little 'kiddies', as she calls them, empty snow out of their boots. She shakes their jackets as well, some of the children look as if they have rolled here, and their coats are all white and furry.

Beth is in the kitchen, of course; she is always there when you need her. She is baking fresh bread and she smiles as she heaves the dough.

"I can't often spend time doing this, in these days of economising, but there won't be too many here today...so I thought this would be a treat. Oh, there's the phone, Miss Heron."

I dash to answer it. It is the bus driver. "I can't get the bus up the hill, I can't get the children to school," she shouts, "I'm ringing from the phone box." Off I go in my high heels, leaving Mrs Dunn in charge. After a few steps I give up trying to keep my feet dry. The pupils are waiting on the side of the road for me, and we walk to school as best we can.

How exciting this all is for the children. We swap stories about our adventures and how we got to school. The more you fell or skidded, the better was your story. It is only half past nine, just think how much more could happen in the time we have left!

I gather all the children into the hall. Miss Sara Faye trips in at this moment wearing a purple hooded coat and purple booties. I am sure this is not exactly what Mrs Dunn meant by stout shoes and overcoat.

"I am so sorry for being late," whispers Sara smiling gently, "the road was really very slippery."

The phone rings again and I dash off to answer it. Mrs Plane only comes in on Mondays and Fridays so there is no one to pick up the phone in the staffroom. Just when I get there, it stops ringing. I am annoyed and phone County Hall immediately to ask for an extension in my classroom. My voice comes out anxious and shrill.

"No problem," came the calm reply, I am taken aback. "I will process your request immediately and will confirm with you when work is to commence." I cannot believe my luck. I pop my head round the kitchen door to tell Beth. Her face breaks into a crinkle as she works the dough further, for our meal.

Beth's lunch is delicious, what could be better than a broth with Beth's bread? There is a cosy atmosphere, the snow links us together against an invisible outside world.

After lunch, it is still snowing, I decide that the children really ought to go home. I ring all the parents and then the bus company to ask for the bus to come early.

I trot along the corridor to Miss Faye's classroom. She has transformed her room, she must have been working hard, it is like an Aladdin's cave. She has labelled books and displays and there are material drapes of earthy colours hanging down from the ceiling. There are labels saying, 'Have you seen our new books?' and 'Look under here'. It all looks so wonderful; I am sure that the Infants really like being here in Sara's classroom.

"Hurry and go home, Sara, it really is getting very dangerous." I urge her to be on her way. "I will take your children in with mine." Then I rush back down the corridor to my room.

"Here's the man who gets you if you don't come to school," shouts Neville as I stand in front of my class. He is over excited, which is not surprising, so I go over to quieten him.

The man is Mr Clarke, the Welfare Officer. I met him at my last school. He is in a jolly mood, his big round face full of smiles. He tells of the dreadful state of the roads and how schools in the villages are finding things exceedingly difficult.

"Have you any problems?" he asks genially, I think he is hoping that I have a snow related story. But I want to tell him about our overcrowded minibus. I am sure that there are too many children coming to school on it.

"Oh, we've had this problem before," he says as if to reassure me, "the parents put their kids on the bus in the morning, even if they haven't been issued with a bus pass, and then, of course, the children think that they can get back on it to go home."

I silently sympathise with the parents because if they live less than three miles away from the school, they are not allowed school transport. But the roads round here have no footpaths and are so narrow it would be dangerous to walk on them safely. However, rules are rules, so I take the names of the pupils entitled to travel on the bus and determine that after this snow has cleared, I will tackle the problem.

Later, I see Sara rushing off, as she waves through my ever -open door. I hear the bang which tells me she is on her way home. After saying goodbye to Mr Clarke and seeing all the children off, I am left to face the hazardous journey in my unreliable car. The phone rings as soon as I shut my front door.

"Hello, is that you?"

"How are you, Dad?"

"Oh, you know."

"What have you been up to?"

"Nothing much, but I've watching the birds and I've been thinking about the starlings you wrote about."

"Are they still crowding your bird table?"

"Yes."

"What a nuisance."

"Well, that's just it I don't think they are a nuisance. Somebody has to feed them. They are all God's creatures after all. I have been studying them and seen how nice they are if you look carefully at their colours. I am calling them 'birds of paradise' from now on."

"You are right, Dad, their feathers are like petrol showing all the colours of the rainbow in the sunlight. I like your name for them."

"Look out for them in your garden, then. Take care in the bad weather."

"I will, Dad."

"Make sure you do. Ta-ra."

The snow stops over the next week, then it starts again. When I went to bed there were just a few flutters, but I am awake sooner than I anticipated.

I hear a noise, a scraping, I rush to look out of the window. It is Bill, my next-door neighbour, and he is standing on my drive scraping the snow away, from behind my car, with a shovel. I open the bedroom window and a swathe of snowflakes hurry in.

"Are you going into school this morning?" he yells.

"Yes," I answer in a more confident voice than I felt. The snowflakes were big and whirling.

"I'll dig you out then," he shouts up to me, and already I can hear his shovel at work again. It is only six in the morning.

I put on my old dressing gown and dash downstairs. Snow falls in when I open the door to a bright white world. I sit down huddling my cup of coffee.

Goodness! What am I thinking of? This is no time for daydreaming, I need to go and thank Bill and I need to ring Miss Faye and tell her not to set out today. The road to Fish will be treacherous. Several neighbours have joined Bill and my drive is soon clear.

I arrive at school and twenty children have got there before me, some have walked, and some have come by tractor. The school bus stops at the bottom of the lane again and I walk to collect five children, this time I am in my wellingtons. Mrs Dunn helps me with the 'little kiddies', and Beth cooks some muffins for playtime. Mrs Plane arrives, because it is Friday; she is reliable and does not live too far away.

I snuggle into my classroom with a handful of children. It is us against the world. At playtime we go out in our wellies, with coats and hoods to build an igloo. There is so much snow we can cut the bricks out with Mrs Dunn's shovel. I am so engrossed that I do not see our visitor arriving.

"So, this is what you get up to when the parents' backs are turned." A clear voice rings in the still air. It is James the Chair of our PTA; he looks so handsome in his long, dark grey tailored coat. I stand there staring at him with the shovel in my hands, flushed with all my efforts. Suddenly feeling rather foolish, I usher the children back indoors to do some more meaningful work.

"It's 'in' time, come in, children," I shout to the reluctant few, who want to stay outside.

"Sin time," shouts Neville and the others echo his call as they run inside, to be attended to by Mrs Dunn.

"I've come to take my little boy, Sam, home – things are getting very dangerous." James dashes off with Sam in tow.

"Close the school!" he shouts. I think that this time, I had better phone County Hall for advice. But the officer who comes on the line says that I must keep the school open despite my descriptions of the roads. I wonder if they know how bad it is out here.

We help Beth set out the tables for dinner in the hall and we are just finishing her warming home-made soup when I realise that Neville is not here. My heart misses a beat. I know that he arrived this morning, I remember him shovelling snow for the igloo with great vigour. But now, thinking about it, I realise that I have not seen him since. No one else has seen him either. What am I to do? Just then a Council worker arrives, blocking any immediate thoughts of Neville's disappearance from my mind.

Apparently, they cannot keep the road open for much longer and they want the bus to take the children home as soon as possible. I have no choice. I phone the bus company and I phone all the parents. I look for Neville's phone number, but his parents do not answer, and they have not given another contact. My nerves are taut, this is scary. It is profoundly serious to lose a child, even one like Neville.

The minibus arrives and my thoughts of Neville are momentarily stopped. There is a new driver at the wheel. He looks a bit unkempt and does not inspire confidence.

"'ello, luv." He grins at me revealing uneven browning teeth. The engine is running, and he leans out to shout at me.

"Where's the 'eadmaster?"

"I'm Miss Heron, I'm the Headteacher." I try to sound dignified and stand up straight to make myself look taller.

"Oh, there was a bloke 'ere last time I came. I have something to say to you." My lips are dry, I try to swallow. I am near to panic; I must get this over with quickly, and search for Neville.

"Well, I got this job, you see and we 'ave to pay Neville's dinner money, so I'll cough up next Friday when I get paid." He winks at me. Oh, my goodness, this is Neville's father. He should pay dinner money in advance like everyone else on Mondays, but I cannot be too high handed, after all I have lost his son.

"Neville is not in school," I blurt out. "I am so sorry; I don't know where he is...I...am so sorry." I am gabbling. I lick my lips. What on earth will he do now? I do not like to be on the wrong side of a chap like this, or any chap come to think when I am responsible for his missing son.

"Oh, 'e came 'ome, luv. 'e got fed up after you stopped building the igloo." He starts to laugh. "Did you think you'd lost 'im? Wish you 'ad. Ha, ha!" He winks at me again. "Come on, let's get going."

So, our little children stumble onto the minibus, a huge Council gritter and snowplough are in front. The whole convoy moves off. Our country bus looks very fragile with its precious load of children and its unusual driver. I stand and watch. Just then Neville comes sledding down the road.

"Whee ee." He just misses the bus and waves to me giving a huge grin as he whizzes past, I jump away so that I do not get sprayed with sludge.

The bus swerves and his dad shouts out of the window,

"Get lost, can't you, Neville?"

February Sunday

Dear Dad,

What snowy weather it has been! We are having fun at school and the children love it. Everything looks so beautiful and on my journey in the mornings all the trees glisten. I don't think you will have as much snow as we are having as you are milder near the sea.

Do you remember the year we had that unusual very bad snow? I thought it was so exciting and wrote it all down in my diary. The best bit was when the school double-decker bus got stuck and you went with the tractor to dig it out. Good job you had towing chains to pull it. I had never seen anything like it before and we had a day off school. I was at the Comprehensive by then, at Ripsea, and was glad of a day at home.

The cleaner here at school has been helpful and she is so kind with the children. Neville, the boy I told you about, has swapped his bike for a sledge, he loves it but is not good at controlling it and we have to make sure we keep out of his way. I don't know which would be safer for all of us, the bike or the sledge.

Rebecca, the shy little girl who does not like PE, has not managed to get to get into school – she probably doesn't feel safe in the snow.

I haven't got a bird table yet, but I am putting bread on the top of the snow, and you can imagine the greedy sparrows come chattering in as soon as I put it out. Sometimes I get a flock of starlings, your birds of paradise, they come in like a black cloud and polish off the food to the last crumb.

Bill and Joyce next door are wonderful neighbours and Joyce often invites me in for a cup of tea after school.

Love Vi xx

Chapter 8

Snow angels

After the weekend, we are nearly all back at school and working hard, trying to concentrate and not think of our snowy break.

"I'm not emptying your bins today, love, I can't get the lorry into your drive it's too risky." I look up to see a big man, in a red boiler suit at my door, disturbing the peace. Beth comes hurrying through the hall, from the kitchen, and peeps anxiously round into my room.

"Miss Heron, what about the kitchen swill? It shouldn't be left on our premises, and we don't know when the lorry will be here again in this weather."

"It just can't be done," shouts the man, now red faced to match his outfit. "Sorry and all that."

Our bins are emptied every two weeks and so I can see Beth's point. It cannot be hygienic for decaying food to be left on the premises for a month. But if the school drive is inaccessible, then how do we solve the problem?

The fiery man stands, with his arms folded and his legs astride, Beth is still hovering with a concerned look. I stand in-between them. Then Mrs Dunn arrives on the scene, she has overheard.

"Mrs Heron, the kiddies should not be on the same premises as that rubbish...and the smell. Well, we only need it to thaw, and it will all be high." I ignore the 'Mrs', for now, as she continues. "If it gets warmer, we are in trouble, if it gets colder there could be more cancellations. Hot or cold we lose out."

Rebecca starts to cry and several girls crowd round her to give her comfort. 'What did Mr Norman do?' I wonder, but there is no mention of him.

The rest of the children are watching, with their pens poised, in the middle of their number work. Who is going to make the next move? I can see Neville leaning forwards, perhaps hoping for a fight.

"Show me your problem," I say firmly as I stride past the red suit. I am wearing my interview outfit and feeling confident.

"I'll tell you the problem, you're wasting my time that's what. I don't know what you all think I bloody well am – Superman or something." The children stare open-mouthed. Even Rebecca stops her sobs to listen.

I go down the corridor and out through the front door, he follows. I can see the difficulty. Mrs Dunn has cleared as best she can but there are still only wheel tracks for cars and the snow has piled up on either side. It would be impossible for the rubbish truck to get down here.

It is then that I notice a second red-clad man sitting in the high up cab of the lorry on the road. I wonder if he will help. I stride out to the road and try to talk to him. He is waiting with a vacant expression, staring into space. His engine in running and he does not hear or see me as I shout up and wave my arms.

"Couldn't you carry the bins up the drive to the lorry?" I venture to the first man. "Just this once?"

"If I do it for you, I'll have the whole bloody village wanting me to carry their bins up drives. What bloody time do you think I'd finish work then? You teachers wouldn't know about that, finishing work at three, like you do. Part-time job I call it."

Right, that is it I have had enough.

"Here, what are you doing?"

I drag at the handle of one of the bins.

I will move these bins come hell or high water, I think, and I roll up my jacket sleeves and take a last sad look at my clean interview outfit. Then I make a more determined effort at pulling the heavy metal bin handle. It is a dead weight, but I heave for all I am worth, and the bin begins to yield. It only moves a centimetre or two, but it is progress. There is a loud scraping as it jerks over the salt lumps that Mrs Dunn has liberally spread. The drag echoes round the white landscape. A thunder roar of defiance.

"Stop! We can't have Headmistress carrying bins." The man in the lorry jumps out, as if activated by an electric switch, he charges down the drive and his mate lopes towards me. They both snatch the bins, as if they are snowflake light, and run with them up the drive.

Finally, as if in their act of defiance, they throw the lids and empty bins into the snow, then drive off as fast as the road conditions will allow. I look up and see some of the children in my class are staring out of the hall window at me. Neville waves and I see Emily arrive and speak to them as they all scurry back to their classroom to get on with their work.

Beth is smiling her crinkly smile when I get back in.

"I'm wondering if your class would like to come up the hill and see the snow drifts, this afternoon?" she asks. I think that after the drama of this morning it would be a good idea even though some of the children will have seen them, others living further away will miss them when the thaw comes. In any case, I think it will make a good poetry lesson for later.

We are ready with our coats on when Rebecca says sadly, "I don't feel very well, Miss Heron." By the pained look on her face, I do not think there will be anything to be gained by forcing the issue. I decide to leave her with Miss Faye, and she visibly brightens as she collects her books and then trots off down the corridor to the Infant class.

"Oh, I do love Miss Faye, I feel better already." She turns to me and waves.

We plod on through the snow with Beth leading the way. Her grass green headscarf showing up defiantly against the landscape in its unaccustomed white garb. Then before I could stop him, Neville suddenly throws himself on the snow and shows us how to make snow angels. He lies down on his back and then slowly moves his arms up and down to make the 'wings'. We love the outline and if it freezes tonight, it will still be there in the morning. But I quickly dissuade the other children from having a go. I do not want them all to get wet and cold.

We plod on to the sight that awaits us at the end of our journey; it is unbelievable. The drifts are so very high and curved like waves frozen in time. As we walk along the ridge, we see that the wind has sculptured and modelled the snow into what could be faces. The children are quick to see possibilities and features not present are soon added – a sly grin, big ears and crossed eyes, so that before long there is a whole row of leering faces lining the track. I stare at the spectacle, but the children want to move on, and we are soon walking precariously along the top of the drifts.

Every now and again a scream goes up into the unhearing sky as someone's legs plunge into a soft chasm. It suddenly happens to me too. I am walking along a firm crusty surface when suddenly, like pushing your finger into nearly set icing sugar, half of my body disappears into the unknown. I am quite helpless until three laughing children heave me out.

At last, it is time to go back, we wave goodbye to Beth, who has led us in this treat and joined us in our frolic. Her house is up this hill and not too far away. I watch her green headscarf as it bobs along and then turns a corner.

On our way back we meet the red bin men trudging down a side lane.

"Our truck got stuck on our last farm stop. Wouldn't you know? Where's the nearest phone box?"

"Oh, come back and use the school phone," I offer, "and I'm sure you'd welcome a cup of tea."

"You're a bloody angel," says the driver. We turn our back on the setting sun, with a sky as bright as the bin men's boiler suits, and head for school. Our long dark shadows race ahead trying to get back to warmth and safety before we do.

February Sunday

Dear Dad,

We are still having fun in the snow. The cook, Beth, took us to where she knew there were some very high drifts, and the children had a real lark.

The dustbin men are having a difficult time getting to the isolated farms. They got stuck and came for a cup of tea at the school and I had a nice chat with them. One was an elderly man who feels he is too old now to do this job, but also too old to try another job and he has a family to support. He says he hates being a dustbin man. But the other one is only a lad really and he wants to be a disc jockey. He runs a bit of a club in Newford Community Hall on Saturday nights.

In the end they were rescued by a Council van, but the bin lorry is still stuck up there in the hills. Let's hope the thaw comes soon!

I still haven't bought a bird table, but I have a makeshift one now. I got a shelf bracket and managed to screw this onto one of my fence posts. Then I got a piece of wood – it looks like oak – I found it in the garage, and I screwed that onto the bracket. So, I have a bit of a table and I can see it from my window. There is an old rose bush growing round it, just briars at the moment, but I am looking forward to the summer when I will see if it flowers.

Anyway, the birds are coming to feed, I have put some more bread out and some bits of leftovers and I have blue tits and great tits as well as the starlings that you get.

I hope your bird table is still doing well.

Love Vi xx

Chapter 9

Things begin to move

Mrs Plane is in school today, it is Monday. I must admit that she is good at her office work, even though she keeps the flag flying for Mr Norman.

When I arrive this morning at eight, I decide that I am going to tackle the cleaner's cupboard. It is full of an assortment of bits and pieces. I want to try and make space for the new delivery which is still piled up in the staffroom. I hope to get it out of here and into the store. Rebecca and Caroline have come in early to help. I take it as a good sign that Rebecca volunteered. She must be getting used to me and maybe be confident enough to do PE soon.

I have a big cardboard box for rubbish. We fill this immediately. Then I find some old wooden rulers, they measure in inches, so they are out of date. We have smart white plastic rulers now which use centimetres. They do not take up much room, but I feel good getting rid of this redundant stock. We work until nine and by then there is a lot of space to take the extra cleaning materials.

"That is such a good job done. Thank you, Rebecca and Caroline." Rebecca smiles shyly but Caroline answers, "I can help you with the parcels that have just arrived, if you want, Miss Heron." I decide that they are too heavy, and, in any case, classes need to start. Caroline goes to wash her hands.

A little later, I discover that the parcels contain some of our new maths scheme. I open the boxes in front of the children. We are all excited and pore over the new books. They are brightly coloured and have funny little cartoon drawings in them.

"Hey, look at this guy," shouts Neville, "he's acting about, I can see he's putting stuff behind his back, right." The children all want to know his page and start leafing eagerly through. So far, we have been struggling along with my home-made work cards and some sections of the older books which were left here.

Thank goodness, that now I will not be working away at night trying to keep the children's maths work going. We have been so full of enthusiasm for our new books that we did not notice Mrs Plane sitting patiently in the corridor. She is obviously waiting for the dinner money. Her big Quality Street tin is resting on the small table in front of her. Her pen is poised over the dinner register. She stares motionless. I bound over to her.

"I am so sorry, Mrs Plane; I didn't notice you waiting for us. Let us know another time if you are ready for us." She does not move or reply but her eyes refocus on her register and her pen twitches in her hand.

I quickly organise the queue. Neville reluctantly stands in the paying line. He stares up at the ceiling with his hands in his pockets. He says he has not got any money, but he will bring it on Friday when his dad gets paid. The rest of the dinner money collection is soon complete with Mrs Plane's usual efficiency.

After settling the children, I rush off to see Sara in her classroom down the corridor. She is in her library area with all her class sitting round on the carpet. The children are all gazing up at her in silence as she talks to them very quietly. When she sees me, she flicks her hair out of her eyes and gives me a lovely smile.

"Good morning, Miss Faye, I wonder if I could have a chat sometime today about your topic work. Perhaps we could spend half an hour together after school?"

"Oh, I was going into town tonight to buy a birthday present for his nibs. It's his birthday tomorrow and I want to go to the new *Bits and Pieces* shop which has just opened. They have some beautiful glass paperweights with butterflies inside." Sara makes it all sound so wonderful with her big eyes wide open and her lashes fluttering. I hope that the bits and pieces are more attractive than those in the store that we have just cleared out.

I assume 'his nibs' is her boyfriend, Tim, and I wonder if he would really want a butterfly paperweight, but then it is none of my business.

"Well then, let's get together after lunch, we really do need to continue our discussions on your topic work." She nods gently and bows her head to speak to her pupils as I rush back to my class. Most of them are in their seats working, except, of course, Neville, who is rushing around and then hissing, "She's here!" He sits down hastily.

At lunchtime I eat quickly again, as I want to draft out a reminder for the Parent Teachers' Association meeting next week. It is a bit soon for me, but the date was arranged by Mr Norman last term. If I get the letter done now, Mrs Plane will be able to type it this afternoon.

Sara Faye is still sitting at the dining table talking to Mrs Plane.

"I'll just get the tea tray, and bring it through to the staffroom," says Sara, giving me a gentle smile.

I go back to the staffroom and eventually Sara flurries in with the tea tray, followed by Mrs Plane. This takes me by surprise as this is a teachers' meeting. Mrs Plane looks at me coolly.

"Mrs Plane, do you think that you could give us about twenty minutes, please." She stands stock still.

"Oh, Beryl won't mind about our meeting, will you?"

"Well, I would like to discuss our classwork in private, Sara. If you don't mind, Mrs Plane..."

Mrs Beryl Plane stands still and stares into the distance.

"At least let her have her cup of tea," says Sara speaking in a sharper tone than I have heard before. She hands Mrs Plane her mug of tea, and she moves off with it, after snatching up her knitting from her bag.

Sara and I sit down.

"Now, how have you managed with your topic, Sara?" I hope I sound business-like after our troubled start.

"Well, we have been side-tracked what with the snow and everything..." To my dismay Sara sounds vague.

"What, exactly, did you finally decide on with your topic. You said that it was going to be environmental, didn't you?" I try to sound encouraging.

"Did I?" she looks puzzled. "Oh, I remember now, but of course we haven't been able to get out into the woods in this weather." She sounds even more vague and is not looking at me, which is unusual for Sara.

I suggest several ideas and hope that she will find something that can catch her imagination. She looks at me with her big cow eyes and 'yes' she is beginning to see some possibilities, so we jot a few things down.

"Bring your amended plans to me tomorrow, Sara, and we can go from there." She smiles.

"Now, this is what I like to see, hard work, even in the lunch hour, well done." James breezes into the staffroom and casually sits down in one of our easy chairs. What on earth does he do for a living? He seems to come and go as he pleases. He certainly seems very much at home here, perhaps it is because of his PTA connection. I wonder if he is a friend of Mr Norman?

As usual he is dressed very smartly and today, he is wearing a dark blue suit and a silk, light blue tie which highlights his eyes. He looks very attractive.

Sara jumps up and offers him a cup of tea. She knows it is white with two sugars. He engages me in conversation bouncing my comments backwards and forward with skill. His huge presence seems to fill the staffroom and all thoughts of our plans are set aside to pay attention to James.

"Ah, well, I can't waste any more time gossiping, see you at the PTA meeting next week," he announces as he heads for the door smiling at Sara. I stand and he turns, looks at me and does a mock salute before he leaves. The children crowd round his huge white car as he revs it up and zooms off down the road.

I take the tea tray back to the kitchen, ready to start the afternoon lessons.

We begin with a poetry lesson. The children do not seem to like poetry even though I have asked them to write a poem about our enjoyable adventures in the snow. They are enthusiastic at first but soon start fidgeting and looking out of the window, with only a few lines written.

Peter puts his hand up.

"What rhymes with 'snow'?" he asks. We all have a try, 'crow' is the favourite.

"But we didn't see a crow," says Caroline, ever honest and precise.

"You don't have to make it rhyme," I suggest, "or even make it completely true – use your imagination." They look blank.

"Did you write poetry with Mr Norman?" I ask.

Emily puts her hand up and kindly explains.

"Yes, but we thought it had to rhyme. He read us some poetry, as well."

I read them some poems by Michael Rosen from my book called *Mind your own business* – there is a poem about a mother counting while the child gets dressed, a common technique used by teachers to get children to hurry and finish a task, it is usually about clearing away at the end of the day. I have never done this.

"Mr Norman used to do this," says Christopher, who loves numbers. "If we weren't ready by the time he had counted down to one, he went to fractions of one."

The children are eager and listening and I read more. I should have done this first. We write a class poem with some rhymes but not many, it was fun, and they relaxed. I read another poem at the end.

To finish the day, I began to read the story of *The Fantastic Mr Fox* by Roald Dahl. They listen in silence. At the end Neville sits there, as if in a stupor, then he says, "Miss 'eron, you know that Mr Fox, right? Well, 'e wasn't half a one."

At home time, I notice again, that there seems to be a lot more children in the bus queue than there should be. It is something that I have been meaning to sort and I will have another look at my list when I have time. I really must put it on my 'Urgent Jobs' note. This could be dangerous if I do not tackle it. I peer inside, when they are all on, and see that they are packed like sardines. Some are sitting on each other's knees, this must be solved once and for all, it surely contravenes Health and Safety regulations, I am uneasy.

But my attention is taken up, now, by the children who walk home, waving wooden inch rulers in the air. Neville is using his as a machine gun. He is 'shooting' everyone as he pedals by on his bike, giving realistic sound effects to go with his actions. Other children are using them as swords and having fights. Rebecca is cowering in the doorway. Neville returns and starts 'firing' at the school walls. I manage to stop him and rest my hand on his shoulder.

"Neville, where did you get that ruler?" I demand in a harsher voice than I intended.

"Mrs Dunn gi me it." He pushes free and speeds off again into the distance shooting the cows in the field as he goes.

Mrs Dunn! Where is she? I march off angrily and bump into her coming out of my classroom.

"Mrs Dunn, why have you given the children the rulers? I threw them away," I bark at her, and we are both taken by surprise at my wrath.

"I didn't know you were throwing them away, Mrs Heron, they were in this box, and I know you are trying to get rid of rubbish, so I thought you wouldn't mind if I gave them to the children. They can do their counting with the numbers and do measuring at home." She sounds so well meaning and plausible; there is no point in telling her that they cannot do measuring in inches anymore and that they are only use them for fighting. But I do glare at her and stand for a moment, with my hands on my hips, before walking away fuming. It did not seem the right time to tell her to stop calling me 'Mrs'. But, at the last minute, I turn around and say, "Mrs Dunn, please do not take things out of the bin that I have thrown away." I do not wait for a reply.

When I go into the staffroom, after marking some of the children's work in the classroom, the sight that greets me is horrendous to my tired eyes. The cupboard has done what it has been threatening to do since I arrived here. It has gleefully burst open, pushed by the demon rubbish inside, knocking the chair over. I flee with my briefcase full of yet more marking.

I am not looking forward to going into the staffroom the next day with its disgorged cupboard to face. But then, when I arrive, I am so grateful to see that Mrs Dunn has cleared it and put the chair against the door again. I go to thank her. Would this be the time to tackle her about my name? I decide against it. She trundles off with her plastic bag in tow.

Sara's lesson plans have arrived on my table. She has carefully restructured her ideas; she is going to study 'Spring' now. There is no lack of depth, and she must have worked hard. Presumably, her shopping trip was short.

My own plans are to study 'Water' with the children, there is so much I want them to do and learn along with maths and English. I have no shortage of ideas but there is always something that gets in the way. I need more time to teach the children. Perhaps we should not have gone out to see the snow drifts.

March Sunday

Dear Dad,

At last, it's a bit warmer and spring is just around the corner. Are you sowing your peas yet? I bet your broad beans are already in the ground. Your daffodils will be in glorious rows I can just imagine their big blooms that you always like. Time to check your dahlia tubers in the garage. I know you dusted them with flowers of sulphur so they should be free from rot.

I have been reading a book to the children about a fox. It is a bit young for some of them, but they all seem to enjoy it. A lot of them are farmers' children so they understand about foxes and about the three farmers who are trying to kill the fox and his family. I am not really sure whose side the children will be on as they know how much damage a fox can do.

Do you remember I forgot to lock up the hens on our farm one night? I was only a little girl and I had other things on my mind, but it was my job, and I should have made sure the hens were safe. But I didn't and the fox came and bit all their heads off. You must have been so disappointed with me, but I don't remember you telling me off. You just seemed to accept the sad situation. I told myself off, of course.

Do you remember me telling you about Rebecca and how delicate she seems, even though she looks quite robust? She is the one that doesn't want to do any physical exercise. Well, her mother told me the other day that she was a 'sugar bag' baby. She was so tiny when she was born that she was not expected to live. No wonder her mother is so careful and worried about her. It is a great credit to her that Rebecca had done so well and is in such good shape physically. It explains a lot for me, but I still wish she would do some exercise.

You will remember how Mam had to look after me, when I was such a scrap of a baby, having been allergic to that teething powder. Aunt Peggy told me that I owe my life to my mam, and I believe her. Who would have thought it, to look at me now? At least I know a little of what Rebecca's mother must have gone through.

My shelf 'bird table' is covered with sparrows every morning now, but I am also getting blue tits and the robin comes, of course. I hope your robin is still visiting and not put off by your birds of paradise.

See you at Easter.

Love Vi xx

Chapter 10

PTA meeting

Two men came at the beginning of the week to look at the roof again and I rushed from the class to discuss the problem once more. It seemed that in no time at all it was lunchtime, and we cleared our work and put the tables out in the hall, the children lined up automatically.

Sara, Mrs Plane and I sat at a staff table. I was absolutely starving, and I could not wait to tuck in. The children could hardly wait to go out to play and seemed to get through their meal as quickly as me. But halfway through their break it started to rain.

"It's 'in' time," I shout to the ones who are trying to ignore the downpour.

"Sin time," they shout as they tumble in with rain spattered anoraks.

The roof is leaking again, Caroline fetches a bucket. She goes to wash her hands, as I contemplate again how bad a big black bucket looks in my room. I hate it and hope the men solve the roofing problem soon.

By the end of the week two more men arrive to look at the roof. They are dressed very smartly, sporting tweed jackets, they are both holding clipboards. I leave the class, to get on with their story writing, and go over to the men. They are building inspectors and look serious, they keep on nodding and taking notes.

Eventually they come back to me looking miserable.

"What's the verdict?"

"Well, we'll chase the firm over the roof panels and get them as soon as possible but look at this wall." I swiftly glance at my class and then go over to look. We can see peeling plaster;

the water is running along from the leak in the hall roof and making its way down my classroom wall.

"It's my opinion that you will never stop the rain coming in, it's not the panels that are causing the leak, you have two problems," says one building inspector and the other nods solemnly.

I glance at my class and see the children getting restless.

"We'll certainly see what we can do." I wonder how many times they have said this. I dash back to retrieve the lesson, but just then another worker arrives, he is the telephone engineer to fit the extension phone.

"Are you doing it now, on Friday afternoon?" I ask, there has been no notification, but I really need this phone.

"Yes," he nods, "if you don't mind a bit of noise while you all work." What can I say? My lesson has finished, and I read the children some more of *The Fantastic Mr Fox*. By the end of the day the engineer has completed his work. Sara brings in a tea tray and admires my new phone.

Mrs Plane is still in the staffroom when I go in, she should have left by now, surely?

"Miss Heron, I can't find the staffing forms." She has the filing cabinet open and there is a bundle of papers on her desk.

"I need to fill one in. Mr Norman always kept them in his desk drawer. I have looked but they are nowhere to be seen. I thought that you may have decided to file them in the cabinet."

Well, I can make a good guess as to where the forms are. They will have been thrown away by me after my whisky. I would not have recognised them and in my over enthusiastic efforts to clear up, I am afraid, these would have gone unnoticed by me. We will have to phone for some more. I bluff my way through, but I do not think Mrs Plane is fooled.

Having failed on this front I decide to phone County Hall to get an update on this leaking roof. No one is there, it is after all, four in the afternoon on Friday, how could I have thought that they would still be working? I leave another urgent message.

At home I flop in front of my coal fire with a cup of tea when the phone rings.

"Hello, is that you?"

"Yes, Dad, how are you?"

"Oh, you know how it is. When I was a young lad, I woke up looking forward to all the jobs I could do. Now I wake up wondering about all the things I can put off till tomorrow."

"Oh Dad. How are you getting on in your garden?"

"I've put some peas and broad beans in. How's that lad getting on?"

"Neville? Oh, he's fine, he enjoys it when there is an interruption to lessons, especially when the building inspectors came to look at the leak in the flat roof."

"You know I've never held with flat roofs, they always leak, no good at all. And I'll be getting my leeks sown soon."

"Not the same leek, Dad."

"Who says?"

"Dad! I'd better be going. I'm preparing for the Parent Teachers' Association meeting tomorrow."

"Just so you know, your flat roof will always leak, they shouldn't have built it like that in the first place. It's funny I can solve everybody else's problems, but I can't solve my own. Now, look after yourself."

"I will, Dad, bye"

"Ta-ra."

Tonight, is my first PTA meeting. I look on this evening with some trepidation. I have not much idea what people do at these get-togethers. I avoided going as far as possible, at my last school.

I was given a list of committee members by Mr Norman. I sent out a reminder to those people, typed out impeccably by Mrs Plane. I have gone along with Mr Norman's pre-arranged date for the meeting that he set last term. I have not heard from anyone except James, so I do not know who is coming, if anyone. Maybe I should have started again and called the meeting for another day and set out my own agenda. Well, I shrug, it is too late now.

Surprisingly, I have not met many parents, apart from the few who collected the children in the snow. I see some mums waiting outside the school each day, but Sara takes the queue of children out, while I see the children onto the bus, and that reminds me, I must make it even more clear to the parents who can go on the bus and who cannot. I will do it first thing next week. I have already written once. I thought that it was all solved, but I notice that, although at first all was well, the number of children getting on the bus has increased again.

There's James' Ford Capri waiting in the school car park. I catch his unmistakable handsome profile as I swing my car round and park next to him. I jump out quickly and rush, in the rain, to unlock the school door, my watch says exactly seven thirty. I put the lights on in the entrance and then in the hall and the whole school jumps with my switch. James stalks in looking business-like with his notebook under his arm.

"Good evening." He marches into the staffroom, sits down and lights up a cigarette. I leave him there and go to the hall and see that Mrs Dunn has put our chairs out, in a semicircle, facing the top table. There are old, blackened tobacco tins scattered about, presumably to be used as ashtrays. I collect them up and drop them in the nearest bin, leaving only one on the top table.

I hear the door bang, and in comes a very worried looking woman. I recognise her as Rebecca's mum. She speaks earnestly and almost in a whisper.

"I hear that Rebecca was crying in school all day. She is a very delicate child, you know."

"Yes, I remember, but she wasn't crying all day..."

"She was a sugar bag baby, you know."

"Yes, I remember you telling me."

"One of the first sugar bag babies – well two really, she weighed just under four pounds when she was born. It's a miracle she survived – one of the first, with such a low weight." I look up anxious to attend to the PTA meeting.

"Oh, don't worry, Mrs Feathers, we will take care of her. I'm sure she knows her own limits."

"That's just it, she might try to do things she is not strong enough to do." I make an effort to look supportive and think about what a difficult time she must have had. But I cannot stay because now there is quite a crowd collecting. I leave Mrs Feathers wringing her hands and frowning.

The room is almost full of an assortment of mums. Some look very homely in woolly berets and jackets, some of them look as if they have knitted their whole outfits. But some mums look young and trendy with high heeled black boots and tight trousers. There is one in a smartly tailored suit, with a silk necktie. She comes towards me with her right hand outstretched. I recognise her.

"Good evening, Miss Heron, I am Mrs Buckingham, an easy name to remember, like yours. For different reasons of course." I smile and release my hand from her tight grip. I know her little boy, Jake, in our Infants, he is always beautifully dressed in matching trousers and jacket. Mrs Buckingham was the lady at the door of the school who directed me to the vicarage when I came for interview.

Eventually we are all seated. I am at the top table with James, then there is Mrs Feathers, who is our secretary. Then there is Mrs Plane, she is our treasurer. She has her knitting with her, I see.

Miss Faye rushes in at the last minute. She is wearing a little red bobble hat with matching scarf and gloves. She sits next to a parent who chats away to her in a very friendly way as if they are bosom friends.

James smiles directly at Sara then clears his throat. "Right, now Miss Faye is here, let's make a start. Welcome everyone, it's nice to see so many of you, it's just what we want." There are nods and murmurs of approval. I wonder how many have come to see me as the new Head. They are not all committee members.

"I would like to welcome Miss Heron to Fish Primary School PTA and I now ask her to introduce herself and give us her credentials." He leans back on his chair, lights another cigarette, and looks at me. They all look at me. Goodness, I had not expected this. I stare carefully at the wood grain of the table and then up and over everyone's head to the back of the room.

"Well, hello everyone. It's lovely to see so many of you here tonight." I tell them a little about my teaching career and about the new maths scheme.

"But you have not come to hear about me; we have lots to get through and I suggest we get on with the agenda." I look at James, he raises an eyebrow, stubs out his cigarette and consults his notes.

I look along the table to Mrs Feathers, she catches my eye and smiles, she looks more relaxed. Mrs Plane is staring out of the window, her knitting is limp in her hand, and now James is in full swing.

"We ought to be deciding on the details of the Summer Sale. We only have a few weeks left to organise everything. I should ask Miss Heron if she want a Sale as we have always done in the past. Miss Heron ..."

"Well yes — go ahead, I approve, if it's a good fund-raiser. Next year I will be in a better position to judge."

"Right," James beams at me. "Let's get down to business. What are the stalls going to be?"

"Excuse me, we haven't read the minutes of the last meeting yet." This is Mrs Plane stopping the proceedings. But James is charming.

"Well, thank you, Mrs Plane, you are quite right, my mistake. Mrs Feathers, will you do the honours please?"

Mrs Feathers reads the minutes with difficulty. She does not seem to be able to read her own writing and keeps stopping to ask what people think.

"Is that right?" She asks, "Is that what you remember?" When she eventually finishes everyone seems satisfied and I am relieved. The spidery records are signed by James with a flourish in thick black ink from his golden fountain pen.

He looks up and catches my eye, his eyebrows raise again, conspiratorially.

"Now, back to business, I would like to go through the stalls, one by one, and see who is prepared to organise them."

As the discussions get underway, it seems to me that everyone takes the same stall as last year. They have done this for years and I am amazed that they bother to come at all to discuss something that is so cut and dried.

"I would like to include some games, and get the children involved." My voice rings out into the hall. What am I saying? I cannot believe I have just offered that. I have enough to do, and I really want time with the children's maths and English lessons. They have not, so far, made the progress I anticipated, I am not really surprised as there seems to be one disruption after another. Even so, I think I would like the children to have some input into the school Summer Sale.

"What sort of games?" asks Mrs Weatherall suspiciously. I do not really know because my comment was just as much a surprise to me as it was to them. I wrack my brain for ideas as I stare at the table wood grain again.

"What about throwing a wet sponge at a head stuck through a hole?" I had seen this on a comedy film. Everyone looks doubtful. James raises his eyebrows again. There is silence. I blunder on.

"What about 'Whack the rat'?" I went to a garden fete, when I was young, and they had this attraction. There is still a silence.

"Well," James leans forward with his hands clasped in front of him, "I think we can leave those games up to you, Miss Heron." He gives me an encouraging smile.

"I would like some posters to advertise the event, the children could help," I venture further.

"We've never had any posters before, why would we need them? We all know about the sale. All of them who comes does, anyway," reasons Mrs Weatherall. Everyone, it seems, is looking down at the floor. James cuts through the uneasy moment and thanks me for my offer.

"Just a few, perhaps?"

"What about the prizes for all these new games?" asks Mrs Feathers. "All the prizes ought to be the same so that there is no quarrelling." The general feeling is that we could give chocolate bars. A jolly looking parent from the front row offers to buy them for us but how many should she get? For a while twenty-three seems to prevail though I cannot see the logic. It is only a moment ago that the idea of games seemed unacceptable now it has taken over the meeting.

"Let's say twenty-six, then we'll definitely have enough."

"I think we'll need some big bars and some small bars. Some games will be harder than others."

"Thirteen big bars, and thirteen small bars then."

"Not thirteen."

"No, it's unlucky."

"Let's go for fourteen of each," says James and it is decided. "Now is there anything else?"

"There is just one more thing," I add, moving my numb feet around to get a bit of life in them, the room has suddenly gone very cold. Mrs Dunn has informed me that all heating goes off at eight in the evening, that is set by County Hall, and she cannot do anything about it.

"Why are we raising this money?" There is silence again and much studying of the floor.

"Very good question, Miss Heron," replies James. He smiles and his blue eyes catch mine. "We have tended to raise money primarily to create a good healthy balance. Then perhaps think of one or two items for the school."

I take a deep breath.

"Well, I would like a computer for the school." Mrs Plane begins to knit furiously.

"Mr Norman said they could make the children lazy."

There are murmurs of what seems like assent and bowed heads again.

"I would like some beanbags, if everyone agrees." This is Sara, speaking for the first time in the meeting. "They would be lovely for the children in our reading corner."

"No, problem, Sara," James smiles at her. "Is everyone in agreement?" They all nod and some smile and turn to Sara.

"No need for a vote then, lovely, thank you, Miss Faye."

"I would like some reading books, the ones we have are very old." I give up, for now, on the computer.

"Is everyone in agreement? What about £200?" They all seem to smile and nod, again.

"Good. If that is all I declare the meeting closed."

Mrs Plane has just finished knitting with her brown wool and has picked up the fawn. She decides against it, as James stands up, and she pushes it in her copious bag. Everyone begins to chatter at once turning to each other in excitement. I wonder, briefly, if they are discussing my idea of a computer. I strain to hear them, but after a while, I realise what the eager chat is about. They are discussing the Sale and in particular the games.

"Chris would really like 'Whack the rat', I remember one church fete I went to..."

"Emily could easily take on one of the more challenging games..."

"Rebecca would love to do a game, I am sure; I don't want her to miss out, but I would want her to be able to sit down if she gets tired..."

The school is freezing now, we all fasten our coats and rush for the exit. James waits while I switch off all the lights and lock the front door. I get home at eleven o'clock and fall into bed.

The next day, at school, I find all the old black tobacco tins on my desk.

"Mrs Dunn, I threw these in the bin, please leave them there, next time." I sound rather bossy, but then I am tired from a long day yesterday.

Mrs Dunn does not answer but hands me an envelope.

"I found this in the bin on Friday and I don't suppose you want that thrown away." Her bosom heaves tightly in her overall. I take the envelope, I am puzzled. I see 'Neville – dinner money' written on it. He must have put it on my desk without saying anything and it somehow found its way into the bin which is always on the side.

"Neville must have brought this," I say, "and just put it on my desk. It must have been scooped up with other rubbish and thrown in the bin. Thank you, Mrs Dunn." She smiles and heaves her hefty bosom again.

March Sunday

Dear Dad,

Not long to Easter now. My makeshift bird table is doing very well. I saw one robin feeding the other, yesterday. The nest must be near, but they are so secretive I can't find it.

The Parents' meeting went well. We had a good attendance and got a lot of business done. Beth, our cook, came. You would like her she is a real country person and supports the school as best she can whatever happens. She used to run a farm up on the hills, with her husband. But he had a heart attack and couldn't carry on, so they retired to a nearby bungalow and their son runs the farm. As she is much younger than her husband, she got on and found work as the cook here.

I have just found out from my infant teacher that Rebecca is Beth's granddaughter. I would never say anything, but they are so different in character. Rebecca, you know, is the one that does not like PE and gives up so easily. She always seems frightened of new experiences. Perhaps it was the circumstances of her birth that has made her like this. You always say 'circumstances alter cases' and maybe this is true here.

We are planning a Summer Sale – a bit like the garden parties we used to have at Gumbalding Manor. Mam was so proud when I won first prize in the painting competition. I was given half a crown. I painted a picture of the wood where we used to play (but were not supposed to).

I am planning to have some games for the children. One I am thinking about is 'Whack the rat'. I used to watch rats running along the piping in our milking shed. I suppose we got used to them as a fact of life in those days.

I bet your primroses are out, they always make a good show. They grew so well in the woods when we were young children, but you were busy on the farm, I don't suppose you had time to go and see them. They will be out in the churchyard now so I expect you will have seen them there when you visit Mam's grave.

Have you got your potatoes in yet? I remember them under my bed when I came last. And I expect you have rhubarb ready by now. I hope that there is still some left when I come. I will make you a pie.

See you soon.

Love Vi xx

Chapter 11

The Governors

Tonight, I am going to get the school logbook up to date, I have brought it home to catch up. I must write about the daily life of the school in the log, but so far, I have not had time to open it. Visitors must be recorded, as well as meetings, and the progress of the children must be noted. The book is dark green simulated leather with a red binding. It has a shiny lock on it. It is locked and there is no key, it is a shame my master key does not open this.

I wonder, fleetingly if Mrs Plane has the logbook key in her handbag, but I cannot wait until I see her again. I break the lock with a kitchen knife and turn to Mr Norman's last entry.

'It is with great regret that I leave Fish school after one of the happiest years in my teaching career. My thanks go to parents, staff, and Governors. But most of all I thank the children, it has been a privilege to teach them.'

I write my own first entry which is not so eloquent.

'I, Miss Vi Heron, have taken over as Head of Fish school.' I continue with the daily mundane details of events copied from my own school diary. It seems a waste of time in my busy schedule, and I wonder whoever will read this.

I also begin to write my first Governors' report. I want to explain to the Governors what I am trying to do and how I am trying to teach the children in a much more up to date and hopefully better way.

I have bought a new phone book for school. Mr Norman left lists of numbers on scraps of paper which are difficult to keep together. Now I have collated all these and added some of my own in this smart navy, leather directory. It looks professional on my office desk.

But when I next go in the staffroom the following day, I see that my phone book is open. There have been several entries added in red biro. I recognise Mrs Dunn's handwriting. Some have been scribbled out and, in some places, she has pressed so hard that she has made holes in the pages. It looks such a mess, but I must tell myself that it does not matter, and she was trying to be useful. Just like she is still trying to be useful by taking things out of the bin that I have thrown away. I know there was that envelope with money in that she rescued but even so, she should surely not still be making her own decisions about what I should throw away.

I have got used to seeing little piles of objects, that I discarded the night before, sitting on my desk the next morning. So, I have taken to putting things in a polythene bag and sneaking them out of school to throw in my own dustbin. I feel like a thief in the night as I tiptoe to my car with my loot. I really must have a word with her again.

Today, I arrive at school even more determined than ever to have it out with her. I go straight to the classrooms to find her, but she is not there. I search everywhere with no luck. Defeated, I give up my hunt and go to my desk in the staffroom to open the mail. I am taken by surprise as Mrs Dunn is in here dusting my telephone very thoroughly. This is unusual as she normally gets this room done first so I can have some private time to get urgent office jobs done before the children arrive.

"Oh, good morning, Mrs Dunn. I'd like to have a serious chat if you don't mind."

"I thought you might want to see me, Mrs Heron." I ignore the 'Mrs' (again) I need to focus on the rubbish issue.

"To be honest, I thought you'd see me sooner."

"So, you know what I want to talk to you about, Mrs Dunn?"

"Well, I know my own age, don't I?" I hear her sharp intake of breath and see her bosoms rise. She rubs even harder on my phone and spits on her duster to get a bit of stubborn dirt off, I cannot help feeling glad that it is not the mouthpiece.

88

"Your age?"

"Yes, I'll be sixty just after Easter. I suppose Mr Norman told you." I had no idea, of course, but that means that she will be retiring at the end of the summer term. Well, well and joy of joys. I need not steel myself to mention the bins and their contents. No need to worry on that score now, she will be leaving; my troubles will be over. No more smuggling of secret rubbish parcels to take to my bin at home. I do not even care about being called 'Mrs' anymore.

Mrs Dunn has now lost interest in cleaning my phone and scurries off, leaving me to think about appointing a new cleaner.

What happens next? How do I get a new cleaner?

Using my new phone extension in my classroom, I phone County Hall to check. I am keeping an eye on the children, which is easier now I do not have to rush off to the staffroom.

There is a moment's silence then, "Yes, that is correct I have just consulted our records. Mrs Dunn is sixty this summer. If you draft an advertisement, we will see that it goes into the local papers. You will need to do this as soon as possible."

I can do that, but I have not much idea about how to interview a cleaner who is also a caretaker. Mrs Dunn lives in the village and despite my difficulties with her, I have got used to her always being here and knowing about procedures, even if sometimes she knows a bit too much.

Rather than worry, I ring the caretaker's department at County Hall, I get assurances that I will have the help I need when the time comes. I am pleased, but I can see that my pupils have finished the task I gave them and need more input from me. I start to hear them read individually and make notes about their progress and where they need help. It is reassuring to be concentrating on the children without interruption.

When they have all gone home at the end of the day, I use Mrs Plane's typewriter to type out a final copy of my report to the Governors. I work carefully. I want to impress them with all the things I have been doing with the children.

When I have finished, I clip my master copy on to the drum of the old ink duplicator and gingerly turn the handle. But the first thing that happens is that the master copy creases. I cannot smooth it out on the drum. Then when I finally manage to get the duplicator to work, the purple writing has a dark line across it of smudged ink. I pour more liquid into the compartment, but it makes no difference, except that my fingers turn bright purple. I plod on, there is nothing much I can do tonight but I resolve to do something about this infernal machine as soon as possible.

The vicar is the first to arrive, he is our Chair of Governors. He sits in my chair at my desk. He spreads out all the documents and then turns to smile at me and I tell him about Mrs Dunn's news.

Mrs Feathers arrives next, she is our correspondent, this means that she takes the minutes like she does at our PTA. Thank goodness I have prepared my own agenda. There is nothing too onerous and everything should be straightforward.

Four elderly men arrive to complete our Board of Governors. One of them is unsteady on his feet and has two sticks to support him. He stumbles at the door jamb and Mrs Feathers rushes to help him and gets him to his chair. One of the men is dressed very casually with an old tweed jacket and a scruffy necktie but when he says, "Good evening, I am Mr Shawell, son of the Lord," his accent reveals, without doubt, that he was educated at an expensive school.

The vicar welcomes us all and begins with an opening prayer. I must say he is a few minutes into his murmurings before I realise that it is a prayer. I was absentmindedly gazing out of the window when I realised that he was asking God to guide the Education Department into making the right decisions. I hastily look down for the next five minutes until the vicar's voice stops and I hear the shuffling of papers.

One of the men suddenly blows his nose loudly on his huge white handkerchief and I recognise him from my interview. He continues a thorough cleaning job wiping his face and moving his head from side to side before tackling his nostrils with this cloth.

I stare fascinated as he emerges red faced but satisfied and then stuffs the handkerchief into his pocket under his belly.

I hand out the pale purple copies of my report and as they are so hard to decipher, I read most of what I have written out loud to them from my master copy.

I want to tell the Governors how easily children will learn when they are interested in what they are doing. I tell them about our exciting new maths scheme, which so absorbs the children and helps them understand numbers. They seem surprised at what I am saying.

"When I was at school, we all chanted our times tables – couldn't go out to play until we knew them by heart." Next, I tell them about our carefully planned topic work with lots of places of interest so we can foster a fascination for science, history, and geography.

"The capitals of the world and the Kings and Queens were drilled into me," comes from the Governor with the big white handkerchief.

I tell them about some new and exciting reading books I have ordered and some I have already bought. Far from stumbling over texts they can hardly put the books down. I do not tell them about Neville who is already fed up with the monster book I gave him.

"I was caned once for not knowing my alphabet, and then when I got home my dad slapped me for getting the cane at school. Never did me any harm." This comment comes from Mr Shawell in his posh voice.

"Headmistress, I would like to thank you for your excellent and detailed report. I think I speak for all the governors here present that it was a most illuminating account." No one comments further.

"It has come to my notice," continues the vicar, "that our tried and trusted Parent Governor, namely Mrs Brown, is resigning from her post because of pressures of work, indeed we have her apologies for tonight's meeting. I cannot stress too much how sorry we are to hear this regrettable news."

He expresses concern over our predicament as no one knows the procedure for replacing her. He says that Mr Norman dealt with Mrs Brown's appointment last year, but that he, the vicar, will endeavour to solve our problems by contacting the correct authorities before the next meeting.

"Next," continues the vicar, "to make matters worse, I have it on good authority that our steadfast and trustworthy caretaker, Mrs Dunn, is soon to retire..." I let the meeting know that the matter is in hand.

"That is most gratifying, it is good to know that our school is in such capable hands. We must now gird up our loins for the onerous task of appointing a new caretaker. We must not be found wanting when the time comes. We must remember the wise and foolish virgins, must we not?" No one answers.

We are now onto 'Any Other Business'. This is good we are getting through the meeting quite quickly, but I am wrong. AOB turns out to be particularly important. Not least because a petition has been sent to the vicar objecting to even the thought of a computer for the children to use at Fish school.

"I agree, computers will just make the children lazy, they will think everything comes that easy – same goes for calculators as well," says one of the men.

"Nothing worthwhile comes easily."

"Hear, hear. Suffer a bit, learn a lot, that's what happened to me at school." I am ready to talk to the Governors about the advantage of computers in the learning environment, but Mr Shawell interjects.

"A word of caution, I don't think we should be so hasty rejecting the use of computers. We have just had one delivered to the office in London. After all, we used one in World War Two so that we knew what the Germans' plans of attack were."

I would like to make a comment now but perhaps not seeing the relevance of the war in school, the vicar hurries on.

"We must file this letter in our Governors' folder which I will duly sign and date first. It is so encouraging to have communications from the children's good parents. It keeps us in touch with the grass roots don't you think?" He leans back and smiles drumming his fingers on my desk.

I really want to discuss this computer problem, but he hurries on again. "No more business to discuss, Governors. We seem to have concluded the meeting, except for one further matter that has been concerning me for some time, and that, Headmistress, is the plaque on the wall of the old school."

It is the first I have heard of a plaque, but I am most impressed by the vicar's description and by the fact that he says it is a veritable part of our school history. Apparently, he wants to ask the new owners of the old school if we can have the plaque back. He thinks it should go on the wall of our present school. There is much discussion about the removal of the plaque, how to preserve it and how to mount it on our wall. Then we discuss, prematurely I think, the unveiling of the plaque. Who is going to be given this honour? We go through the important people we know.

"The Chief Education Officer?" Surely such a small task for such an important person.

"The last Head of the old school?" I wonder if she is still alive.

"Mr Norman?" Would he want to come back and face me?

"Our vicar?" Well, I suppose it was his idea.

"A parent?" Maybe Mrs Buckingham is suitable with her queenly name.

Me? No one mentions me, and after all this discussion I wonder what would happen if the present owner does not allow us to have the plaque, then all this talk is a waste of time.

Lastly, we arrange the date for the next meeting.

I get my educational diary out as do two other Governors, but it seems impossible to agree on a date. No sooner do I write down 'Governors' next to one date than there is an objection,

'Isn't that the date of the village bingo?' or there is some vague idea that there is an event on that day if only we could remember what it was. Then there is the date that 'rings a bell' but the reason is elusive.

Finally, we do agree on a date and the diaries are put away, notes are piled up and tucked under arms and it is permitted to look at our watches without seeming rude. Then, "Oh no, we can't meet on that night. It is the Young Farmers' Barn Dance and the ladies will all be doing the catering." We wearily make a stab at another date.

When everyone has finally gone it is 11pm. I switch off the lights and lock up, no James to stand guard this time. Strangely, I find that I miss him. I reflect on the meeting, and I wonder if we have achieved anything tonight to further the education of the pupils.

I do not go straight home but I drive to the old school and pull up in the crumbling playground. The new owners, clearly, have not managed to get started on the renovation work.

I take my car torch and walk round. I am looking for this plaque that has caused so much interest and has taken so much of our time at the meeting. I am keen to see the uplifting message that will be on our school wall for years to come. I scramble in the darkness through the undergrowth, my torch casting a drunken light as I lurch around trying to avoid the briars catching my interview outfit. At last, here it is, the stone tablet above the main window. I step back to read the inscription which is just visible beneath the moss and lichen. It reads –

'SUFFER THE LITTLE CHILDREN'

March Sunday

Dear Dad,

The meeting went well, I was glad to meet the Board of Governors at last. They seemed impressed with my report and listened to it carefully. I talked to them about getting a computer in school. It is early days yet, but I do think that they are the thing of the future. I'm not sure you will agree because I know that you did not like the calculator, I gave you. You have always done all your arithmetic in your head and had no use for a machine. But computers can do things we cannot do easily or quickly in our heads. After all, it was a computer that helped us win the war and saved thousands of lives, as one of our Governors reminded us.

Also, there will hardly be any use for paper, so they say, once we are all using computers. In any case, it is a tool I think that the children should have at Fish school. I will still teach times tables and spelling, you will be pleased to know, but I don't want the children here to be left behind in the modern world.

The buds on the blackcurrants you gave me are just beginning to swell. I planted them down the garden in a row next to my neighbour's fence. I have bought some fish at last. I bought five goldfish and they look very good swimming about in my pond, even though I did not have much time to clean it all out properly.

I can see some daffodils coming up in my garden, I bet they are later than yours – the buds are still green and tightly shut but they show me that spring is well on its way. Then there is that Lenten rose I bought Mam; I wonder how that is doing – it should be flowering soon. And how are your cabbages? I imagine that you still have a few that have overwintered. You always manage to grow such healthy vegetables; they are something to look forward to.

We are going to have a plaque from the old school put on our new building. You will know the quote, I should think – 'Suffer the little children, and forbid them not, to come unto me: for such is the kingdom of Heaven'. It is only the first four words that are on the plaque, but I think that you will like it. Jesus wanted everyone to be as innocent as the children. Mind you, I wonder sometimes if all these children are that innocent!

See you next week.

Love Vi xx

Chapter 12

That bus queue

On my way to school this morning I stop to get some petrol. I arrive five minutes later than I usually do. What a difference five minutes make. I find myself rushing around trying to get my science lesson ready. This lesson involves separating salt from water and separating sand from water. I need the equipment to be ready for the children.

It is raining and I see that the leak seems to be getting worse. The big black bucket, put there by Mrs Dunn, is already full of water.

I rush through to the corridor where Mrs Plane is waiting with her tin. It is exactly nine on Monday morning.

We are just singing 'Morning has Broken' (Neville's choice) in assembly when the phone rings. Mrs Plane continues bashing out the second verse as I dash off, noticing all the heads turn as I rush to the staffroom.

It is Mrs Brown the Parent Governor. The one who is leaving because she says that it takes up too much of her time.

"Have you got a moment, dear, or are you too busy?" she continues before I have a chance to reply.

"You'll have to do something about the school transport, they are making such a fuss in the village. I'm not going to name names, but those whose children have had a letter from you about not being allowed on the bus are upset and they mean business."

"Yes, I understand," I say when I finally get a word in edgeways. "I can see their difficulties, but they are not eligible to go on school transport. I had to tell them about the County rules. They are not my rules, and we must obey them for insurance purposes, one of their children could be seriously hurt."

"Well," continues Mrs Brown, "I hear what you are saying, but there's going to be real trouble, I just thought you ought to know. Mr Norman allowed them on, there was no bother with him."

"Thank you for letting me know, Mrs Brown, but..." I do not say anymore as the phone has gone dead; Mrs Brown has put the phone down. She is angry, but what am I supposed to do? It is not safe to pile all those children on the bus. The thought of a deputation of parents worries me a little and my heart begins to bump at the unfair mess of it. I go back to the assembly in the hall making a mental note to call the Welfare Officer as soon as I can.

The children are sitting in silence, Miss Faye is there with her class and Mrs Plane is standing in front of all the children with her arms folded. As I approach, she goes back to the piano, and I smile my thanks.

"Mrs Plane, I would like you to type and duplicate a copy of the letter reminding the parents of our Summer Sale. And I need another letter sent to the group of parents who are not eligible for school transport, please."

"I don't know how I am going to do it; this duplicator is getting worse. Mr Norman did everything he could to sort it out, he even took it home to work on it."

Whatever he did, it obviously did not work, it was a real nuisance when I was trying to duplicate my Governors' report. I understand Mrs Plane having difficulties.

"I'll see if I can get anything done about it, Mrs Plane." She does not answer but gets on with her typing.

At lunchtime I ring County Hall (they are going to tire of me soon). I tell the resources department how old the duplicator is and how we are struggling to get it to work. I am in mid-flow with my hard luck story when I am immediately offered a new one. I can hardly believe it.

"We are going to get a new duplicator, delivered this week," I tell the two women triumphantly. Sara smiles but Mrs Plane frowns.

"I can't believe it. After all the work Mr Norman put into that machine – it's just going to be replaced – thrown out. How wasteful."

At the end of school I watch, with dismay, the huge queue at the front door waiting to get on the little bus again, but before I can intervene, I see that I have a visitor. It is Mr Clarke the Welfare Officer. He has had a letter of complaint from Mrs Buckingham, saying that the bus is seriously overcrowded. Well, thank goodness for that, a complaint from a parent goes a long way. Her son, Jake, does not travel on the bus but never mind she has brought help, I hope. The children start piling on as usual and Neville's dad is revving the engine.

"Stop!" I shout. "We need to check the eligible children again." Rebecca is sitting in a seat on her own.

"I can't do PE next week; I have to see the doctor." She smiles at me; I am relieved that I will not be trying to coax her for a day or two. But I have something more important to solve at present.

Mr Clarke takes out his notebook and the children who should not be there are asked to get off the bus. It sets off with its correct load. I have six children, left in school, ready for home but no transport.

"What do I do now?" I ask Mr Clarke.

"Oh, don't worry," he smiles a jolly smile. "I'll write to the parents of these children, and I'll write to Mrs Buckingham and say the problem is solved." He gives me another big smile and is off with his notebook tucked under his arm. His problems are solved, but I have to get these children home. I ring each set of parents in turn and tell them that they must collect the children from school. But of course, many are busy and cannot come immediately.

I wait and look after them as the grim-faced parents call, one by one, to pick up their offspring. By 6.30pm all the children have gone, at last, and I too can go home, hoping that the bus problem is solved.

At home, the phone rings.

"Hello, is that you?"

"Yes, how are you, Dad?"

"You know – fair to middling."

"How is your garden going?"

"Not bad, but you know I've got too much fruit and too many vegetables now your mam is not here. She loved vegetables."

"Yes, I remember, she thought they were healthy, she even drank the juice they were cooked in."

"I'll have to chuck some."

"That's a shame, Dad. Why don't you give some away?"

"I might stop growing them altogether. Do you remember your mam used to cook nettles? I might do that – I've plenty here."

"You never liked them, Dad – I remember them – they had a strong taste. But Mam used to say that they were full of minerals."

"I think I'll have a cabbage with my beef tonight. I'd better get cooker on."

"OK, Dad, see you soon."

"By gum I'm looking forward to that. Ta-ra"

Chapter 13

Preparations

It is the Easter holidays, and I cannot wait to get away. On Saturday morning, I hastily pack a suitcase and set off to see Dad. The five-hour journey is tedious, but I have several stops along the way. I ring him from the last service station.

"Not long now, Dad, I'm at Ferriby."

"About half an hour then?"

"Oh no, I think it will be over an hour before I get to you."

The last thing I want is to rush or him to worry. I set off again at a steady speed. I roll into the drive of his bungalow mid-afternoon. He is looking out of the window. He has parted the net curtain and seems to be staring into space. At first, he does not see me arrive, I wonder how long he has been standing there watching and waiting. Suddenly, he jumps into action as if by an electric shock. He is at the door before I have managed to get out of my car. He rushes and gets my case from the boot.

In no time at all my stuff is in my old bedroom and we are sitting down next to the fire with a cup of tea.

"What do you want to eat?"

"It's too soon for me, I ate some sandwiches when I stopped last time." We are a bit awkward with each other, as if we are strangers.

"I start getting it ready by now," he says. I decide to go along with him, and I wander into the kitchen.

"What are we going to have, Dad?"

"Anything that is there." There was nothing there except a small tin of beans. I dash off to the shop and get some sausages. We have some potatoes stored in his garage from last year, they are old and wrinkly but are edible with the tin of beans covering them and of course the sausages.

"Sausages are full of sweepings up, you know." He always says this, Mother used to smile and tell him to stop being so daft. But she is not here, and I don't feel like saying what she always said. She sometimes gave him a playful punch as well, but I do not feel like doing that either.

We spend the rest of the week working. I fit into his routine and settle into the reassurance of his home, amongst the furniture and ornaments that I know so well. It is comforting and we lull ourselves into a familiar pattern. I catch up with the housework and shopping and Dad spends his time in the garden. It all looks very tidy with not a weed in sight and the brassicas all in a row. In the front garden his bushes are pruned within an inch of their lives.

"My last day tomorrow, Dad, what do you fancy doing? We can go anywhere and do anything you want."

"I'm alright here."

"What about a picnic?"

"Aye alright."

"Where to? We can go anywhere."

"We'll go and see your mam."

I presumed he meant the graveyard, but I did not ask. I made some cheese sandwiches and filled my flask with tea. I packed the rug that I gave Dad at Christmas and we set off for the churchyard in Gumbalding village.

And now we are sitting amongst the cold graves, the tombs of ancient times, and there is the grave of my soldier cousin who came back from the Second World War having served in Burma. He had developed tuberculosis and although he tried to resume normal life and plan a wedding for his fiancée, he never really recovered and died two years later. I am not sure this is a good place to be.

"He should have had a war grave, you know; it was really the war that killed him. Your mam needs a headstone."

"I'll get on to it, Dad, and find out the prices and get back to you."

102

We did not eat all our sandwiches, but the tea was warm and sweet. I watched a blue tit carrying nesting material into a hole in the old gate post. Preparing for new lives amongst the dead old ones. Dad watched it too,

"Life goes on, but sometimes I wonder what it's all about." We sat staring into the distance at a loss for words.

I tumbled back into number ten after my trip to see Dad. A few weeks ago, the thought of seven days at home with no school seemed like an eternity. I would be able to do unlimited jobs at home. In fact, I had been saving them up, thinking that I could solve everything in the Easter holidays. I have been putting jobs off for weeks now and would soon get them done without having to go into school.

Of course, it did not work out like that, and I could not feel inspired to do much at home. After a day or two I went into school. I found that here I could get on with the jobs easily. I could work on those mundane tasks much better without the children to teach.

I planned my next term's work, and then I sorted out the staffroom cupboard, at last. I was feeling good and virtuous. I packed everything in boxes and put labels on all of them. If anything did not fit into a category, I threw it out. The effect was marvellous. I could now open and shut the door with ease and there was no sudden threat of burial from the contents spewing out.

The last job I did in the holiday was to hire one of those industrial carpet cleaners from a firm called Action Man. I discovered that the name was apt as you needed to be a person of action to even move the machine. It was so heavy and not easy to manoeuvre. I had such a difficult job to get it out of the car and drag it to the offending carpet. Then trying to decipher the 'easy' step by step guide to sparkling carpets was a mammoth task even before I started cleaning.

It did a good job though. The purple monster of a carpet began to smell sweeter, at last. I also comforted myself by the fact that heaving this machine around would surely do wonders for my figure and I could end up looking like Sara, after all. Things were falling into shape, but soon it was back to the school term with a jolt.

One good surprise is that the rest of our new maths scheme for the Infant class arrived. Sara and I opened it together and she was excited as we looked in the parcel.

"These books look lovely. They are so inviting. Look at the pictures and the colours. I cannot wait to use them. I will take the teachers' manual home tonight, even that has pictures in." It was nice to see her so enthusiastic about the scheme, especially as she confided that maths were not her strong point.

Once term started the children in my class began to prepare for the Summer Sale in their break time and lunchtime. They are so excited about it all.

Neville wants to be in charge of the 'Throw the sponge' stall. I have been concerned that he would not like the cold water, but he is not to be deterred. He has painted a large monster on a board and his dad came in one night to cut a hole where the head should be.

His dad looks taller than he does sitting on the bus, he sidled in giving me a lop-sided grin. He had tools in a cardboard box.

Neville rushed up to him and told his dad what he wanted. He did not reply but did the job in a few minutes and then disappeared.

Neville is going to put his head through the hole and then for 5p you can throw the sponge at his face. There is no winner, but Neville says he will shout, 'Good shot', when someone makes a direct hit. At the end he will decide who can have a chocolate bar. The thrower must stand at a distance to be marked out by Neville.

Rebecca has decided, after careful thought, to oversee a game where people guess the weight of a baby doll, carefully made by Mrs Dunn and filled with beans. It was, apparently, her mum's idea and will ensure that Rebecca can sit down for most of the afternoon. People will come to her, to take part.

Emily is planning a treasure hunt, using it as a mathematical exercise with co-ordinates. Christopher, who is good at maths, has helped her, and she has already got her bar of chocolate prize and has wrapped it up in gold paper. She buries this in the sand tray and the children are trying it out already. The chocolate treasure already looks worse for wear and has needed to be replaced several times, as it has mysteriously disappeared.

Caroline has decided to do 'Name the dog' as a fund-raiser. Emily's mother, Mrs Taylor, has knitted the dog. Whoever guesses the name correctly gets the dog as a prize. Mrs Taylor knits at a ferocious pace and has already offered a whole swathe of knitted toys for the white elephant stall.

Christopher has organised the 'Whack the rat' game. His father has fixed a drainpipe on a vertical stand and Mrs Dunn has put a face and whiskers on an old sock. Whenever they can, at playtimes, the children persuade Christopher to drop the rat in at the top and they try to whack it with a roll of newspaper. The rat is already looking decidedly dead.

We are making posters to advertise our sale and individual stalls. We had long discussions about where best to pin these. I have seen notices pinned in some very unusual places. One is on an oak tree on the side of the road where there is no path, as the writing is so small there is no chance of reading it as you drive past in the car.

Caroline has put hers on her barn door and Rebecca put hers up in the post office. This was a very sensible place except that I have been told by several reliable children that she has put the wrong date on it. I have not pursued the matter further as we all know the date anyway and I know how easily she can get upset.

Much to my dismay, I then notice one poster with a spelling mistake on. It must have been one done at home, and I do not recognise the writing, but it says, 'Summer Sail'. I just hope that no one spots it, maybe I should have taken it down or corrected it. But I drive on past and determine to use this in my spelling lessons.

Several children have put their notices up around the school, which is not much use really but at least they have achieved something. They all seem proud of their efforts and have tried hard with the wording.

'Can you afford to miss this?'

'A chance of a lifetime'.

'Get rich quick'. Surely that should be 'quickly'? I let it stand and again choose to ignore it.

I have got used to the posters, but the children never tire of their inspirations and go into fits of giggles every time they pass one. They have had fun and perhaps they have learnt something along the way.

Raffle tickets have also been going out to the families all week. We have had prize offers of a sack of potatoes, a duck and a wastepaper basket made by little Jason's uncle who is in prison. Sara kindly says it was not his fault. Mrs Dunn has made a Kermit the Frog puppet. Mrs Plane is still knitting.

The phone rings shrilly shaking me out of my musings. It is an angry call I can tell.

"Caroline will not be in school today, Miss Heron. I set off to walk with her and by the time we had gone a few yards, we were soaked. It was so dangerous; the cars were almost driving into us. We got so dirty too, what with all the mud on the soft verges at this time of year."

I could not get a word in edgeways, as she drew breath, because she started up again.

"This new system is just ridiculous..." She began to sob. What could I say? Caroline is not eligible for school transport.

"They ought to be made to walk our roads themselves, then they would see what it was like." By now she can hardly get the words out and I can hear the tremble of her lips.

I suppose by 'they', she means County Hall officials. There is nothing I can do about it except listen and sympathise and to say that, of course, Caroline must attend school.

Caroline eventually arrived an hour late in her 'spare' school uniform.

"We had to change our clothes and get washed before we could set off again," complained Caroline's mum. She was wringing her hands in distress, but I was pleased to hear that her husband had brought them in to school in their van.

"He'll just have to bring us every morning and pick Caroline up at night," she sighed. "It won't be easy though."

Caroline looked immaculate, as ever, in her little green outfit. We do not have a school uniform, the children come in what they want, within reason. Caroline's clothes stand out amongst the rough and tumble of the rest.

Mrs Plane saw my newly arranged cupboard for the first time today. I have been looking forward to this for days. It will surely meet with her approval. Everything is so tidy, and the boxes are clearly labelled. Her job will be so much easier now. I cannot think how she managed before, with all that tumbling mass of miscellany.

"I can't find anything in this cupboard, now," is her first retort as I enter the room. "I could lay my hands on anything I wanted before and now I am looking up and down labelled boxes all the time."

The children are excited, and I am finding it hard to keep them on task. The sale is tomorrow, and they can hardly resist practising their games at every opportunity. I content myself with the fact that they have been, practising giving change with our carboard coins, writing for the posters, working together and co-operating. Everything is ready.

Then Peter, whose father's farm adjoins our sports field, comes running back after school.

"Miss Heron, Miss Heron, my dad says that we can have pony rides round the field tomorrow." His face is bright red, and he is out of breath, bending over to regain composure. He holds his hands on his legs and his head is down for a few minutes.

"What a wonderful offer, Peter, but who is going to supervise all this?"

"My mum and dad – they said they would." He looks up at me pleadingly.

"Thank you, Peter, that will be lovely and please thank your mum and dad." He runs off muttering his own gleeful thanks.

Now, to get the hall ready for the sale. A bombardment of mothers, complete with energetic toddlers, arrive to help set out the stalls for tomorrow. Before long, the little children are laughing and crying and running up and down the corridor. Older children in their excitement are taking a forbidden slide across the hall floor.

"Where do you want the stalls, Miss Heron?" I have no idea so I say, "Put them where they were last year and then we can see how the games fit in."

To tell the truth, I cannot see how anything can be arranged in this hubbub, but James strides in to help and has clear ideas of what to do. I am grateful for his steady hand. Slowly but surely, under his direction, the shape of things to come becomes clear. It is all beginning to look good, but then I spot that the little children have started to play with toys arranged on a table for sale tomorrow. James notices too.

"Thank you, ladies, I think we are as organised as we will ever be." He speaks firmly and everyone knows it is time to go home, no matter what stage they are at in their preparations.

"Oh goodness. What about the refreshments?" I gasp when they have all left, except for James. "Where do you usually have them?"

"We usually use your room but it's full of children's games. Damn, I'd forgotten all about that." He wheels round on his heels looking for a space.

"What about the Infant room?" We both go down the corridor and look, yes, with a bit of furniture removal it will be fine. Mrs Dunn appears, rushing around with her black plastic bag. She looks disapproving and takes a sharp intake of breath.

"Don't do the cleaning tonight, Mrs Dunn, it isn't worth it. There'll be quite a lot to do tomorrow after the sale." I hope I sound grateful in advance, as this is a lot of work for her, and I am not sure about extra overtime payment.

"We've never used the Infant room before," says Mrs Dunn with another quick intake of breath. "Mr Norman would have a fit if he knew." She hurries off, and a good job too, I think she would be surprised to hear my view on what Mr Norman would think, at this stage on a Friday evening.

I go into the staffroom, at last, to pick up my briefcase and notice a letter on my desk along with the poster with the spelling mistake.

'I spotted this and knew that you would want me to report to you. You know how badly this would reflect on the school. Please let me know if I can assist you further. Mrs L. Buckingham.'

At home, the phone rings.

"Hello, Vi, is that you?"

"Hello, Dad, how are you getting on?"

"Fair to middling, what's your weather?"

"A bit cold tonight but we've had a clear day. What about you?"

"Cloudy all day with a west wind. What's new?"

"I have rung the stonemason near Hull, the one that you told me about, and he will give you a quote for Mam's headstone."

"How much?"

"Well, it depends on how much writing you want and if you want a picture."

"What sort of picture?"

"An engraving, lots of people choose flowers."

"Aye, that sounds about right."

"Do you want me to ring him again?"

109

"No, I'll go tomorrow — then I'll say what I want. How are you getting on with your sale?"

"Really well. There are lots of people willing to help."

"How's that lad getting on?"

"Neville? He loves it all. I think he will make a lot of money for us."

"Make a good businessman then?"

"He could do if he concentrates — he's certainly got the courage. Have your swallows come back yet?"

"Yes, I've opened the garage window and they have been in and out. Your mam used to see them from the window."

"Did she like them?"

"Not much. She wasn't a bird watcher you know — she wanted to do her embroidery and then when she couldn't do that, she liked quiz programmes on television."

"Oh, she was so good at embroidery."

"She was and she worked for Madame Clapham, you know, and embroidered for royalty. Ah well, I'd better be getting on. Ta -ra."

Chapter 14

Summer Sale

The day of the sale has arrived, at last, and it is quite a mild day, thank goodness. I am driving along my country road when I spot the heron again. He flies close to my car, and I can see him so clearly. He flies in front of the windscreen almost near enough to touch. I notice his bright eye and the black and white head, then his long, kinked neck. The slow flap makes him look as if he has all the time in the world, but he has not because I have become so mesmerised that I am going to hit him.

I take my foot off the accelerator and press the brake as hard as I can. The wing tip feathers fold on the windscreen, I close my eyes. But there is no awful sound of the thump of a body against the glass and when I squint out again, I see him, still in his unconcerned way, journeying slowly into the distance.

I turn into the school car park, hoping to be the first to arrive but, no, there's James' Capri. He gets out of his car before me, and I rush to unlock the school door. I am very aware of him as I fumble to get the key in the lock. The door opens outwards and as I step backwards, I bump into him, He hold his hands up. "Oops," he smiles. My heart misses a beat.

The hall begins to fill alarmingly. I suddenly wonder how many people we are supposed to allow in the hall to be in-keeping with the fire regulations. But it is a fleeting thought because in no time at all the children rush in and tumble over themselves to get their games organised. They start playing them immediately.

The vicar has just arrived. I can see him over the crowd, and I squeeze my way sideways to go and speak to him. He is going to open the sale for us. According to Sara people usually start buying as soon as they arrive, but I wanted something a little grander and more formal. However, I have seen today that people have not waited for my grand opening, they are, indeed, buying as soon as they get here, or asking for the best things to be reserved. I am not going to change things overnight; I tell myself for the umpteenth time.

It is half past two and time for action. James is standing by me with the vicar. I ring the hand bell.

'Clang! Clang!' Everyone stops and looks around in surprise at this rude interruption.

"Ladies and gentlemen," I begin as some chatter on. I raise my voice. "Welcome to the Summer Sale at Fish school. I will now ask the vicar to do us the honour of opening the proceedings."

I begin to clap as he moves slightly forward with a fixed grin on his face. A few people nearby join in the clapping, and I see that Sara does too, with her dainty hands and pink nail varnish.

The speech begins and the vicar's voice reaches a few bystanders at the front, but the rest of the crowd eventually give up all pretence of listening and turn their backs to get on with more important business. They ignore my loud 'Sshh...' but the vicar will not be cut short.

"...what a pleasure it is to see so many of my parishioners here today and may I take this opportunity to encourage you to endeavour to attend Church on Sunday when we will be having a special family service..."

I do hope that he is not going to go on for ages, but I am afraid that he does, and I give a sigh of relief when I finally hear –

"... and so, without further ado, I declare this Summer Sale well and truly open." No one is paying attention, but Sara comes and kindly offers a cup of tea. No one claps, they are all too busy at the stalls.

I go over to the children's games. Neville has set up his 'Throw the sponge' game near the front door. Everyone who comes in gets wet and brings their footprints into the hall. Mrs Dunn, in her short wellies, is trying to stem the flow of puddles in the entrance, with a mop and bucket. She is taking so many sharp breaths inwards she will surely blow up like a balloon very soon. I hear her trying to persuade Neville to move, but he is having none of it.

"Come on, Neville, just move a little way down towards the car park, please," I add to Mrs Dunn's remonstrations.

"They won't see me there, right, I won't be able to get 'em all before they go in."

I go over and begin to lift his contraption and he with a shrug helps me, we gradually move a little way along.

"Come on, have a go." He shouts at another group of children coming out to see what is going on. They start pelting immediately. Neville whoops and gets into position, and I begin to wonder if he is charging anyone at all or if it is all just developed into some different sort of game, with Neville as the star attraction.

Mrs Plane is in the staffroom, she is knitting in grey with large needles. Her big, sweet tin gapes open and empty in front of her. Her profit and expenditure sheet is drawn up with careful precision waiting for her neat and accurate numbers of credits, debits and balance.

"Come and have a look round, Mrs Plane, there's no money to add up yet." I do not like her sitting on her own like this with all the fun going on everywhere.

"Oh, you'll be surprised how soon it will come in and then I won't have a minute to spare for hours, I can tell you. I know from experience." I still cannot understand why she needs to sit here and wait, but I say no more, she knows what she is doing. I leave her stoically guarding her empty tin.

I wander over to the children's games. They seem to be a great success. But Rebecca's 'Guess the weight of the doll', is an exception. Perhaps no one wants a knitted doll, I muse. Mrs Dunn has made it so carefully; it is worked with a little knitted dress and yellow shoes and hat to match. These days I suppose that it cannot compete with the Cabbage Patch dolls which all the girls here seem to want.

"I'm bored," complains Rebecca. Well, I am not surprised that she is not getting much custom, her sad face will not tempt anyone to come near, even if they did have a passion for knitted dolls.

"Let's see if we can find a friend to take over for a while," I encourage. But no friends seem to be forthcoming. Emily is sympathetic, but she is really very busy with her queue of people wanting a go at finding her treasure. As I leave, Rebecca gives a loud sigh and crosses her chubby arms over her chest and stares down at her shoes.

It is then I spot Sara in the crowd. I watch her heading towards Rebecca and I see her pick up the doll and take it round the room. She is encouraging people to have a go. Rebecca, suddenly free, makes her way to 'Whack the rat' and vents her anger on the dilapidated specimen, with great vigour. I am thinking that this cannot be good for Rebecca's health. I glance around for her mother, but she is nowhere to be seen. I look once more and then decide to move on because Rebecca looks as if she is enjoying herself and seems no worse for all her efforts.

At last, the sale seems to be over. The stalls are practically empty. The children have finished their games. But no one wants to go home. I have been sauntering around smiling for about three hours.

The refreshment room is still full of people chatting and eating. Beth's cakes are so tasty, and the prices are so low that no one can stop buying them. Beth, with a smile on her face, keeps on bringing laden plates from the kitchen.

How do I signal an end to this sale? I have a sudden vision of us all smiling, eating, and chatting well into the night, with Peter giving pony rides by torchlight. Mrs Plane would be counting her money for ever.

I catch sight of James talking to Sara in the crowd, he is smiling and standing a little too near, I notice.

Suddenly and on cue Neville arrives.

"There's no more that wants a go with 'itting me with a wet sponge, right, so I packed me board up, right?" He fishes in his wet trouser pockets and brings out hands full of 1p and 2p coins. They spill onto the hall floor. Children start scurrying after them and stamping on them to stop them rolling. Neville's pockets are still bulging, the weight is beginning to pull dangerously at his trousers.

"Well done, Neville," I enthuse. "Now, take it all to Mrs Plane in the staffroom, please." He swaggers off with his trousers already at hip level and his vest hanging out.

"About time we had the raffle in'it, Miss 'eron? Some of us 'as to get back to see to our animals. We can't hang about here all night." This is Mrs Weatherall, speaking harshly.

To be honest, I had forgotten about the raffle. We go over to the table where the prizes are set out. Someone has been so careful. The table is covered with an ironed white Damask cloth. The prizes are arranged as if they were as precious as the crown jewels. Most of them are knitted animals which Mrs Plane, Mrs Taylor and Mrs Dunn have had a hand in. There is also Mrs Dunn's carefully sewn Kermit the Frog. It is sitting in pride of place in the centre, propped up by the bag of potatoes.

James comes over with the bell and rings it vigorously. He winks and smiles at me. Sara is nowhere in sight now.

"Right, ladies and gentlemen, this is what you've all been waiting for, the grand draw. Have your tickets ready please." There is a shuffling and scuffling with pockets being turned out and handbags being searched. Then there is silence as expectant faces look towards me.

"Which do you think should be first prize, Miss 'eron?" Mrs Weatherall asks me, with a flick of her blond hair. This is a tricky decision. I try to work out who would cause me the most trouble if their prize is not seen as the most important.

"Weren't we supposed to have a duck for one of the prizes?" I venture to ask by way of diversion."

"I'll get it. It's in the corridor," shouts Mrs Weatherall above the increasing hubbub and agitation for us to get on with the raffle. I can see the anticipation on people's faces.

Back comes Mrs Weatherall with a wooden box. There is wire netting on the top and a loud quacking coming from inside. The poor duck is still alive. It is a mallard given by Mrs Edwards from the hills. I had fully expected her to kill a duck and bring it plucked and drawn, ready to be popped in the oven. However, no one else seems taken aback and James hastily asks the vicar to pick the winning ticket out of a bag.

"Number 261," he shouts. He holds his hand out to me for the prize. I have no time to deliberate further, and I plonk a red elephant in his hand. I hope no one takes offence but I hear Mrs Dunn's sharp intake of breath behind me. All the prizes are useless really. Everyone seems to have a fixed grin on their faces but what is happening now? They look down, staring at the floor and there is silence.

"Pick again," I say with a determined smile.

"Number 98." There is still no claimant and no name on the ticket. The ghastly truth is beginning to dawn, no one wants the red knitted elephant. The vicar picks a third ticket and this time a little girl shouts and we all clap, with relief, as she comes to claim her prize.

A man with a cheery smile wins the hapless duck.

"I only came in to use your toilet and was persuaded, at the last minute, to buy a raffle ticket. I'll throw it back in the brook on my way home," he grins.

At last, some people are beginning to drift off, we do seem to have come to an end. My legs are weak with tiredness, but there is all the clearing away before I can dash off.

I have a lovely surprise though, because the clearing away seems to be done in a jiffy. Mrs Weatherall is soon standing with a big plastic bag full of the few unsold articles from the stalls.

She has scooped up what is complete rubbish and should never have been brought here if you ask me. There is a broken lampshade, a dress with a hole in and old books without spines. Mrs Weatherall is apparently taking them to Oxfam. "Waste not want not," she says. "It's my motto."

In the staffroom Mrs Plane has added up the profits.

"How much have we made, Mrs Plane?" Even my tiredness disappears in the enthusiasm of the moment.

"Well taking off all the expenses the total is £395.64."

James puts his hands in his pocket and sorts out £4.36.

"I always like a round number, we have raised £400," he says with a proud flourish. But Mrs Plane is none too pleased because that messes up her figures. The rest of us are smiling and pat ourselves on the back for such a good result.

At last, we can all leave, it has taken us so long that it is almost dark outside. I should be used to this by now, but I am tired and find it hard to get the key in the door to lock up. Then there are steps to negotiate, and I slip. Suddenly, Sara is on one side of me and James, on the other. Sam trails behind.

"Come on, Sam," James calls and then with a toot of his horn he is off into the black hills.

The weekend is bliss, but all too soon it is the back to the work routine, and I drive to school looking out for that heron. I am still elated by the amount of money we raised at the sale. I rush to the kitchen and tell Beth of the triumph; she is all smiles.

"Just think £400, isn't that wonderful?" I enthuse. Beth is so kind and chuckles with the fun of it all. But when I go to the staffroom the Profit and Loss account, which has been carefully typed out by Mrs Plane is on my desk. It says that the total raised is £399.84. I rush to find Mrs Plane who is waiting for dinner money with her empty tin. I query the figure with her, why isn't it £400 as we agreed?

"Oh, it turned out that the expenses were just a little more than I calculated," she says without expression.

"But what about James? It meant so much to us all to reach that magical sum of £400. I would have given you the 16p to make it up."

"You should have said," is her reply as she turns to her dinner register without expression on her face.

May Sunday

Dear Dad,

Things are going well here. Our Summer Sale was a great success. It seemed that everyone in the village came to help support the school.

You should have seen Neville – he got wet through with his game, but he seemed to enjoy people throwing a wet sponge at him. Everyone said what a good sport he was. Rebecca, the sugar bag baby, did a game as well. She didn't raise much money but that's not the point it's the taking part that counts, isn't it? Emily guessed the weight, mind you I think she had quite a few goes to be kind to Rebecca. Emily forgot to charge people for her own game, no wonder it was popular! All the prizes which were chocolate bars seemed to disappear very quickly.

We made £400, which was a record and a credit to everyone's hard work.

I have to think about getting a new cleaner now that Mrs Dunn is retiring. I am sure that there will be a lot of villagers who would like the job.

Have you had the quote yet for Mam's headstone? Did you manage to see the stonemason? We can talk more about it if you want on the phone. No hurry though. You know that I will help all I can.

I wonder if you have any fledgling blackbirds on your lawn yet. I must have a nest here because I can see the male and female blackbird searching for worms today. They cram their mouths full then fly off to the hedge at the end of my garden.

Talk to you soon.

Love Vi xx

Chapter 15

Great minds

For some time now I have been receiving applications for the job of a new cleaner. It is going to be difficult to choose. All the forms, I have so far, are as bad as each other. The applicants do not seem to have tried very hard to answer all the questions on the form. A lot of the replies are cursory and many of the questions have big blank spaces after a short sentence or two.

I have received references for the five candidates I have chosen. All of them sound like good honest citizens and there does not seem to be much difference between them. If only they had filled in more details on the form, it would maybe have been easier.

To my dismay Joyce, from next door, has applied for the post. She has been such a friend since I arrived at Oak Rise but, obviously, I cannot choose her just because I know her. I must remain impartial.

Villagers have been having a discrete word in my ear for the last two weeks. I have been quite shocked that the parents think that it is a decision for the village. Mrs Weatherall even came up to whisper that one of the candidates was rumoured to have had an unmentionable disease, 'down below'.

"Nothing that I can prove, mind you, but it's what they're all saying. I don't know if we would want someone like that with young children. You know what I mean, Miss 'eron?"

I decided to take all the application forms home and work on them from there.

Then this morning, Mrs Dunn came bursting into the staffroom soon after I arrived.

"Mrs Helen Field would make a good cleaner. I know for a fact that her own house is clean and she's a hard worker." I remain silent.

"I just thought I'd put a good word in for her."

"Mrs Dunn, I'm sure I don't need to tell you that the whole matter is confidential, it is up to the Governors to make their decision."

She takes an exaggerated intake of breath then continues unabashed, "Well, what with you being new here, I thought you ought to know these things. You can't be too careful with little kiddies, can you? You couldn't do better than Mrs Field, you know." I turn away.

Suddenly, a man staggers in carrying our new duplicator, it is in a big brown box with a picture of it on the side. Mrs Dunn is galvanised into helping. She tears the cardboard off and clears all the packing away. Then she picks up the old duplicator.

"I'll get rid of this for you, Mrs Heron." She carries the machine as if it were as light as a feather and scurries off with it.

I am quite cheered by the sight of the new gleaming orange machine and am so pleased that County Hall has not let me down. The instructions are clear, I can easily work out how to use it. It is such bliss that I only need to turn the handle and the paper feeds itself through. The type is bold and even, on all copies; it is much clearer than the old one.

"Mrs Dunn," I call. I have had an idea. "Can you take the old duplicator into my classroom, please?"

My idea is that the children could write and publish their own newspaper. They can use the old duplicator and we need not bother Mrs Plane.

All the children crowd round as Mrs Dunn heaves the duplicator onto a table. They are eager to try it out and are thrilled at their results, even though the pages are often smudgy and sometimes indistinct.

"We need suggestions for the name of your newspaper, if you are keen to write one." Keen? They are falling over themselves with enthusiasm.

"Fish and Chips."

"Pick of the catch."

"In the net."

"Fishy stories."

"Heron News."

So many titles come tumbling out only to be discarded and another one is thought of. 'Fish School News' seems sensible, but they are not easily convinced.

They could not wait to start. Caroline is appointed as editor, they thought she was so reliable and hard-working. Everyone is given a job, there is to be a sports page, a joke page, a recipe page, and a puzzle page. At the last minute they remembered that there had better be some news. I thought that Neville would be in charge of the jokes, but the children chose him for the sports page. He qualified because he rides a bike to school. His prowess with a bike gives him great kudos. It is lunchtime before any of us stop for breath. Caroline finally agrees to the paper being called 'Fish School News'.

I take the tea tray into the staffroom. Mrs Plane is going to duplicate some work sheets for my older pupils.

"The new duplicator will make life much easier for you, Mrs Plane," I say with genuine enthusiasm.

"Oh, I'm afraid of it. It looks so modern, I'm worried that I'll break it." She speaks quietly, looking out of the window.

"The instruction book is quite easy to understand. I can go through it with you if you want. But I'm sure you won't have a problem."

"But the old one was like an old friend to me, and I could use it easily. This one is so complicated by comparison."

"Oh, Beryl, I feel the same, but I will help you if I can." Sara has just arrived in the staffroom.

We all sit in silence drinking our tea. I love new things and long to move the school on. But when Mrs Plane gets her knitting out, the wool is black. The conversation moves to knitting patterns. I have no idea about knitting so cannot join in.

At present she is knitting a scarf and the pattern is very intricate. She knits her life away as Sara watches.

In the afternoon, the older children are getting on with their maths, while the younger children are story writing, Mrs Plane comes into my classroom. She begins to use the old duplicator. I watch as she slowly and determinedly feeds in each individual sheet of paper. I think of the new, all singing all dancing, machine in the staffroom.

"I can't get used to the new one," she shrugs.

At the end of the day, I turn my attention to the interviews. I decide to interview all the five candidates and Mrs Plane has another go with the new duplicator. She seems to be getting on well with it now. Sara breezes in, apparently Tim's Headteacher, Miss Nelson, has bought a new photocopier instead of a new duplicator like I have done. It was Tim's suggestion. They are getting on well with it and the only disadvantage is that it uses electricity which Miss Nelson thinks is a waste. They are all limited to five minutes use before it must be switched off to save money.

I wish now that I had waited and asked for a new photocopier instead of this duplicator. Things are changing so quickly these days, no sooner have you bought a piece of equipment than it seems that it is out of date and has been superseded by another idea altogether.

Mrs Plane shrugs and carries on.

The phone rings when I arrive home.

"Hello, Vi."

"Hello, Dad. How are you?"

"Fair to middling, you know. I've been thinking."

"What about, Dad?"

"About your mam's clothes. In her wardrobe."

"What do you think?"

"Well, I know some people pack them away, but you can't just pack your mam away, you know, as if she had never been here."

"What then?"

"I'll sort a few things and give them to the Red Cross; she liked them. And I'll get rid of old stuff, she wouldn't have wanted anything out of date. But I'll keep the rest. I like her clothes hanging here. She was always so smart, and, by gum, she was good looking."

"She was, Dad."

"How are your fish doing?"

"Really well, I love watching them and they come up for food when I throw pellets in the pond."

"That's good. Let me know who gets your cleaning job. You won't get such a good one as the one you have now."

"I will do my best, Dad."

"Ta-ra"

At the end of the week, it is time for the interviews. The vicar arrives as I am clearing up the classroom.

"I'm afraid that you are in an invidious position, Miss Heron. I hear that your close friend and neighbour is one of our applicants for the vacancy."

"Well, no, not really. Yes, she applied but the best person must get the job. She will be given the same chance as everyone else but no more."

"I admire your pragmatism, Miss Heron." He shrugs and examines the wall suddenly, with great interest.

"The school could really do with decorating, after all it is ten years old," he comments. "It is extraordinary how the County justifies its economies. I was only speaking to the other day to the Deputy Education Officer about such matters. He is a most intelligent and deep person..."

I have already thought about this, but do not want to go into details now. I am too concerned about the forthcoming interviews to worry about the state of the school paintwork at present. I smile vaguely and go into the kitchen to make tea. He steps behind me. Then our Chief of Caretakers suddenly appears and joins us.

"Now, take me, for instance. I came from nowhere. I started on the bottom rung as plain Mr Smith." We had hardly got over the introductions before he launched into his origins.

"I know what it's like to be a nobody but look at me now. I've kept my nose to the grindstone and worked my way to the top." I pour a cup of weak tea, matched by my hesitant smile.

"I'm no snob, but when you see the youngsters of today, well really!" He is encouraged by the vicar's nods. "They're not prepared to put their backs into things. And the way they dress, well!"

I pass him a tea and then one to the vicar who announces that he is not averse to partaking. They turn to each other and begin to chat. I leave them absorbed with themselves to see to the candidates who have already begun to arrive.

Mrs Dunn has put chairs for them in the front entrance and there they sit. All very upright with feet together and handbags on laps. The candidate with the alleged questionable disease has withdrawn so that is one less complication. The phone rings but before I can get there Mrs Dunn answers it from my classroom. She tiptoes in with a note on a scrap of paper. Joyce has withdrawn there is no explanation. In a way it is a relief, but I hope it is not because of putting me in an awkward situation.

When we are all ready, I call in the first candidate to the staffroom which is our interview room.

She can hardly speak and seems overawed and dumbstruck. Her tight skirt rides up her thighs as she leans back. The hem of a droopy grey petticoat slithers out between her legs. She cannot answer anything but promises all. She is eager to 'help the little ones'.

Next, we have Mrs Helen Field, she is in her twenties and looks about sixteen. She is wearing a Laura Ashley purple dress and it really suits her. The big gold earrings dance a jig round her neck as she talks. She is sure she could learn to operate the heating system if she is shown how, the boiler is always a worry to Mrs Dunn.

The vicar is keen on the heating system, and he thinks that we should all be engineers in case of an emergency.

"Are you going to produce children?" he asks. "This is a very important question as we may appoint you, and then you could become pregnant and have to leave us." I really do not feel that he should be asking this impertinent question, also he did not ask this of the last candidate. I feel that I should say something, but Mrs Field says that she would eventually like to have a child. How sad, I think, for her to have to disclose such personal information.

"Hopefully, but not for some time." She answers confidently and her earrings dance around her smiling cheeks.

Our last candidate has jet black hair cut short into a bob, which she has pushed neatly behind her ears. Everything goes well until she discloses that she could not possibly come in the mornings as she has two children and must take them to the High School, which is several miles away in Newford. She wonders if we could get round it by bringing her two teenage lads with her in the mornings, then dash off to get them to school in time for the start at nine o'clock.

"They wouldn't be trouble," she assures us, "they could watch telly or do some crayoning or help me."

At last, all the interviews are over. It is not a contest really; there is only one possible candidate. But the Chief of Caretakers wants to tell us what he thinks.

"Well, I've got a lot of experience in these matters, and I pride myself on being a good judge of character. The first candidate is out of the question, and I didn't like the third one, so I go for Mrs Field. She is a good cheerful character."

"If I may be permitted to speak," says the vicar, clearly affronted that he did not get to have his say so first.

"I, myself, am fully acquainted with all these characters. You also must remember that everyone in our little community knows them. Our village people, quite rightly in my opinion, have an idea of who deserves this coveted position of caretaker. You must both consider these factors carefully and weigh up these matters before you decide. Now, I have made careful notes and I wish to go through them with you..."

He continued for a few minutes then finally says, "and after careful consideration I wish to appoint Mrs Field."

Then the Chief of Caretakers gets up and shakes the vicar's hand vigorously.

"I am so glad that you agree with me. I can tell you that my considerable experience serves me in good stead, and I was able to identify the correct candidate immediately."

They forget to ask my opinion.

Of course, Mrs Field does seem to be the best candidate. I could work with her, and I am sure she would get on with the rest of the staff here.

"I am in favour of appointing Mrs Field," I say loudly and clearly.

"Go...od," hums the vicar and turns to the Chief of Caretakers. "You won't regret it, mark my words."

I go outside to tell the candidates of our decision, but to my dismay no one is there. They have all gone home. I shall have to phone them with the news. It is a bit of an anti-climax. The vicar hurries off, but the Chief of Caretakers stays and sets about inspecting the school for dust and dirt. He lifts the carpet and runs his fingers along high rails. Mrs Dunn appears and carries on mopping with her sharp intake of breath. She comes within centimetres of his spotless black shoes with her rag mop.

"A word, Miss Heron, in the privacy of the staffroom, if you please." He beckons me and marches off. He sits down and I close the door.

"Now, as you can guess, I have found hidden dirt in the school, but my advice to you is that we would not want to upset

Mrs Dunn, the incumbent, at this stage. So, when Mrs Field eventually takes up office, I will accompany her around the school and spell out details of our requirements." He flaps the pages of his cleaning manual in front of me. I feel sorry for Mrs Field.

"I can see that I am going to get on well with that young lady. Now, I must be going as I have an urgent appointment. If you have any further need of my advice, I will be only too willing to help." He marches off and gets into a big flashy new car and swoops off.

I phone the candidates with the news. Mrs Field is so excited that I expect her to pop down the phone line any minute. Mrs Dunn comes to find who I have appointed.

"You won't regret taking my advice, Mrs Heron. It is the right choice." She bustles off, probably not wanting to think about the fateful day when she must leave the school.

Alone in the staffroom, I write a letter to the parents asking for a donation to Mrs Dunn's retirement present and tell them about the new appointment. Then, I write to County Hall asking if we could decorate the school ourselves using the new County Aid Scheme. I have read about this recently. The County supplies all the paint and the community do all the work.

I have just finished the letter when James pops his head round the door. He has come to see who we have appointed as cleaner.

"Good, good, you have made the right choice there," he nods and smiles at my news and takes a step towards me, with his arms held out. Forgetting myself I step forwards. I can almost feel his arms around me. Just then Mrs Feathers arrives and asks for a word.

I ask her into the staffroom and James jumps away and grimaces over her head as she sits down. I wait for him to leave. He shrugs and goes out. I hear the front door bang.

"What seems to be the matter, Mrs Feathers?"

"Well, you know that computer thing you want for the school. Well, if it is easy to use and you don't have to walk about to get books and things, and you don't have to work hard..."

"Yes, yes." I have not got the energy to go into the advantages of a computer at this time of night, but it certainly is not to make things easier for the children.

"Well, I think that it would be just the thing for Rebecca – her being not too strong. She could learn her lessons without using much energy if you see what I mean."

I have a convert for the computer, at last, even if it is for the wrong reasons. I glance at the clock.

"Well, I think that we should ask the Education Office to buy us one straight away, the sooner Rebecca gets on one, the better for her health," she says. I explain that it does not work like that and that we are given 'Capitation' which is money to buy equipment like pens, paper and books each year. I do not add that I have already spent most of it because of the new maths scheme we needed.

"The money is not enough to buy a computer and County Office does not have a separate fund for one. The PTA did not want to fund one, so we are stuck for the time being."

"Well then, I am going to start a computer fund. It would be such a relief to me to know that Rebecca could use it whenever she wanted." I decide not to explain just yet that there are another fifty children in the school that will also be entitled to use it.

"I'm going to start with a jumble sale, at home." Her face brightens as she starts making notes in a little book about how to raise money. I usher her out as soon as seems reasonably polite. But to my dismay I see Mrs Buckingham waiting to have a word and all thoughts of an early night disappear.

When I finally get home, Joyce is standing at my door. She has her apron on and she holds her arms out to me.

"Oh, Vi, here you are. I am so sorry to let you down at the last minute. What must you think of me?"

"It's alright, Joyce, we had plenty to choose from. Everything went well. Please don't think any more of it." "I intended to come; I really did want the job. But I applied to work in the shop here, as well, and out of the blue this morning they phoned and asked me for interview. By this afternoon they had offered me the job. I had to take it. I am so sorry."

"Nothing to be sorry about, Joyce. I am so glad you got a job."

"I didn't want to embarrass you." She shivers in the evening air. We hug and arm in arm we rush for a cup of tea in her house and then I settle in for a quiet weekend.

May Sunday

Dear Dad,

I hope that late frost did not catch your potatoes, I saw there was one due but maybe it did not get to your plants. You said that you'd planted the red Duke of York. I remember they are your favourite since the war. I wonder if the red colour makes them taste better.

My fish are doing well in my garden pond. I managed to clear it out a bit more, and it looks much bigger, so I bought some more water plants. I am very pleased with my efforts.

The children at school have written a newspaper and each one has taken a copy home for their parents. They are so enthusiastic. It is a way I can get them writing without even trying, they have even stayed in at playtime to fill their pages.

I am making progress with getting a computer for school. A parent is starting a fund and having a jumble sale. Then a parent called Mrs Buckingham told me last night that she has already bought a computer for her son Jake, who is in the infant class. She is so thrilled to be ahead of the game and has bought an expensive model. But the good news is that she is having a coffee morning to raise money for our own school computer.

Mrs Buckingham likes to do well by Jake and takes him to all sorts of historical places at the weekends. He is always coming up to me to tell me about where he has been. The other day he said to me, "I went to a 35 house yesterday." I didn't know what he meant but the Infant teacher was there, and she knew.

"Oh, Jake, you went to a fortified house, didn't you? An old house that is a fortress as well."

"Yes that's it 45, not 35."

He had got the wrong idea altogether!

Computers cost a lot of money so I expect that it will take us a long time to get to our target. I appointed a young woman from the village as the new cleaner. I am very pleased and so is Mrs Dunn as she is the one that recommended her.

I wonder if you are already picking your gooseberries, they are always early, I hope you will make a pie.

Love Vi xx

Chapter 16

The swimming lesson

On Monday when I arrive at school, I notice that the plaque has been put up near the front door. 'SUFFER THE LITTLE CHILDREN'. Not a good omen, I think, but the vicar is there talking to the parents, and they smile at him.

"I must declare that I did all this single handed. All the organising that is, our most esteemed builder Mr Jones is very handy with a drill, under my supervision of course."

"What about the unveiling?" I remember the discussions at the Governors' meeting.

"Oh, I think we can dispense with the ceremonies now. I gave it a blessing yesterday when I was proceeding to the church." The little crowd of mothers disperses, and I go inside.

Mrs Dunn takes a sharp intake of breath when she sees me. What can be the matter? Is it because I did not choose her frog as the first prize, I wonder? But I have no time to worry about this for long because today we are going swimming. We are going with the nearest school, two schools on one bus, so that we can reduce costs for the County. My pupils are excited about their swimming lesson with Bridlypool Primary School, the series of sessions is a once-a-year expedition.

The bus is late, and the children are difficult to keep quiet in the queue outside. They swing their fluorescent swimming bags with impatience. Neville's is swinging so high that it eventually hits Christopher. I calm them both down before I race to phone the bus company. I have just begun to dial when I hear the smooth purr of the coach engine.

I rush back to find that the children are crowding round the door but when they see me, they get back into their queue. The driver opens the bus door and I let Emily in first as she has volunteered to carry our crate of swimming floats and arm bands. I had hoped that Rebecca would help, it might have given her more confidence, but she could not be persuaded.

The town coach is bright red and silver inside and out. We have never seen anything like it before, so different from our little cranking country minibus that comes to school each day. The bus driver is not Neville's dad, he is a big silent type and is wearing a maroon uniform. The seats are so high that I cannot see the children when they sit down, and you would not know that anyone was there, apart from the occasional bright bag swinging in the aisle.

Off we go at last along the narrow lanes to Bridlypool, where Miss Nelson is the Headteacher. Sara's boyfriend, Tim, is the other teacher. Apparently, Tim normally comes for the swimming lessons, but he is taking the children camping this weekend and has a lot to sort out.

I have arranged all the details of our swimming trip with Miss Nelson over the phone. I must say, I am looking forward to meeting a colleague and sharing some of my thoughts and some of my worries with her.

I can see Miss Nelson and a parent, who is to be our life saver, with the pupils waiting in an orderly queue on the grass at the side of the road. We stop outside her school. It is a little red brick Victorian school which, like Fish, has only two classes. The automatic door hisses and folds back, but no one moves. Then I hear laboured breathing as Miss Nelson's head appears in the stairwell. She is wearing a furry hat in the style of a hedgehog. Her large square face is red and expressionless as she slowly climbs the steps. Her full figure rises into the coach. Her smart grey mac is tightly belted around her ample waist and is matched by her stout shoes. Miss Nelson stops and surveys the bus seats as she catches her breath.

"Which side are the Fish children occupying?" Her town crier voice is demanding attention. Is she talking to me? Which side? What does she mean? My children just sat where they wanted, I did not know that we had to have sides. There is silence, while she walks along the aisle of the bus looking at the children. I stand up and find my voice at last.

"Hello, Miss Nelson. I am Vi Heron." I hold out my hand. She ignores it and stares over my head, without moving and my hand slowly drops.

"On which side should the pupils from Fish school be sitting?" she demands.

"The children just sat where they wanted. Wouldn't it be nice if the children mixed and got to know each other?"

"According to my information they have not done so on previous occasions," she replies through gritted teeth. "It will make the rules more difficult to enforce and disembarking will be a problem. However, as you have already seated your children, I will not countermand your instructions."

She beckons her children who are still waiting patiently in their queue.

"Come along, Bridlypool children." She shouts in her sergeant major fashion and assists all her pupils as they climb the steps, putting a gloved hand under their left arms to help them. The children seem to accept this without a word and allow themselves to be propelled onto the bus. When they are all safely seated, she is quite out of breath and stands heavily for a short while. She then goes down the gangway checking that everyone is settled.

"Will the child from Fish school occupying the front seat be so kind as to move?" shouts Miss Nelson from the back. "I intend to sit there. I do not want your company and I do not suppose, for one moment, that you want mine."

I am quite disappointed; she seems so old fashioned. I had great hopes of having cosy chats with a colleague and friend in the nearest school.

"Hello, Miss Heron, so nice to meet you." She takes me by surprise and this time she is looking at me.

"How are you getting along, dear? Not drowning in a sea of paperwork, I hope. I do not open most of my letters, I file them in the round bin under my desk. If it is urgent, they'll write again." She plonks down on the front seat breathing heavily and taking time to arrange herself and get comfortable. I am on the seat behind her, and I lean forwards to catch her words which are tossed over her left shoulder.

"Have you filled in the questionnaire about which English scheme we use in school?" I blurt this out suddenly, it is something that has been on my desk for a few days. Every morning when I arrive there it is; I have been worrying about it. To tell the truth I don't use a scheme, I teach English as part of everyday lessons and plan a focus each week.

"Oh, I expect I put that in the green, round filing cabinet, under my desk, again. I advise you to do the same. They can always come and see for themselves, I have not the time to do their work for them." She rearranges her handbag and gloves into the small space left on the remaining seat next to her overflowing body.

"We use *Better English* – books One to Five. The children start at the age of five and work their way through them until they leave school. You see…"

I am afraid that I cannot hear any more because I fall asleep. It is a combination of her monotonous voice and the humming motion of the bus that seem to have done the trick.

I don't think that Miss Nelson notices my indiscretion, though, because when I wake up on a sharp corner, as we turn into the swimming pool car park, she is still in full flow. She is anguishing about the children's inability to spot the difference between 'their' and 'there'.

When the coach driver finally manoeuvres into the tight parking space, Miss Nelson gets up immediately.

"Now, all the children on my left, stand up… I said left, Amanda, don't you know your left from your right?" She turns to me and makes a loud 'tut' in disgust.

"Now off the bus smartly, this side only." Everyone obeys, including me, and in no time at all we are in line and ready to go into the building.

Miss Nelson changes into gleaming white gym shoes and dons a huge wrap-over pinafore. It is the type that goes over your head like my grandma used to wear. Holding onto her handbag, she strides onto the poolside area. I came in my tracksuit, with my swimming costume underneath, and I go into the pool area barefoot. Rebecca is sitting on a bench reading her book.

"Oh, Rebecca, why aren't you getting changed?" I ask in surprise.

"I can't go in, Miss; I have a verruca." She should have brought a note, but she waves the offending bare foot in my direction, and I can see that she does have a big black round verruca and so is not allowed in the water. I am disappointed and thwarted yet again in my aim to get Rebecca taking more physical exercise. She smiles and settles down to read her book again.

"I'll take the swimmers, Miss Heron," shouts Miss Nelson and in jump the swimmers at her command. Their task is to swim round and round as she swings her arms in the required direction. She encourages them by shouting, "Swim, children, swim," in her loud confident voice. She continually counts the heads as they bob up and down because 'you can't be too careful'.

My lesson is composed of a series of exercises to get the non-swimmers more confident in the water. I have various activities for the children to practise and for them to have fun. Of course, my children get excited and make much more noise than Miss Nelson's group and when one of them splashes water over the side and wets her pinafore she glowers at me.

We are getting towards the end of the session and Miss Nelson has already synchronised her watch with the clock on the wall several times, when suddenly I become aware that all is not well.

"Swim, Amanda, just swim. Swim for goodness' sake girl!" Miss Nelson's voice is beginning to show a degree of alarm. I glance over to her group; Amanda seems to be finding it difficult to swim at the deep end and is thrashing about helplessly. I blow my whistle and all the children get out; we have talked about doing this in an emergency.

The children quickly leave the pool, except for poor Amanda, of course. She is now taking gulps of water as she comes up to the surface every now and again. I look hastily for help, but the parent, who is our life saver, is at the shallow end, momentarily distracted by the children on the side of the pool.

Miss Nelson seems to have backed away, so I have no choice. I pull off my tracksuit and quickly slide in. I tread water and Amanda grabs my outstretched arm. Then she panics and puts all her weight on my shoulders. I go under, taking Amanda with me. I kick rapidly and we surface to take air.

"It's alright, Amanda, I've got you." I hold her head out of the water and she gradually calms down.

The life saver parent, who by now has arrived on our side of the pool, holds a pole out for us. We both grab it and are soon safely on the pool side. I look for Miss Nelson, but she has her back to me and is issuing sharp commands as she ushers the children out urging them to hurry and get changed. It is then I realise to my consternation that I have not remembered to bring my own swim bag with underwear and towel. Emily kindly lends me her towel and I dry off as best I can.

Back on the bus, the maroon clad bus driver gives me his newspaper to sit on as the water is seeping through onto my tracksuit trousers.

Maybe our plaque should say 'Suffer the little children... and teachers'. Miss Nelson does not speak to me but turns around frequently to berate one of the children for some minor misdemeanour. I am just too cold and miserable to say or do anything.

136

The bus stops at Bridlypool school and all the children alight in perfect silence. I sit glumly looking through the window, wishing again that I had a friendly colleague.

Then, just as Miss Nelson has helped the last child off the bus, I feel a strong squeeze on my shoulder.

"Thank you, my dear," she whispers in my ear. "I'm afraid I did not know what to do when Amanda got into difficulty. It is good to know that I have a trusted friend and colleague at Fish school."

And with that she heaves off the bus and instructs her troops back into school.

Chapter 17

Secrets

On Monday morning I arrive at work early as I want to get on with some more lesson preparation. James' car pulls in immediately behind my car, my heart does a leap.

"Vi, what's this Community Aid Scheme all about? I read the letter you sent home with Sam."

I tell him as much as I know, as he follows me to the staffroom, for some reason my heart leaps again. He really is very attractive.

"Good idea, good idea." He is pacing the room smoking and absentmindedly flicking his cigarette ash on to the floor. It is a good job Mrs Dunn cannot see him, she has lost none of her pride in keeping the school tidy, even though it is nearly the end of term.

"Look, why don't we get the Parent Teachers' Association to organise it? We need a meeting this Wednesday to discuss Mrs Dunn's leaving present." He seems agitated and his pace quickens. "Good. Right. You've started a collection for her gift, haven't you? Right, see you."

I have no time now for that extra preparation. I snatch my book of assembly stories and instruct the children to line up to go into the hall. Sara is already there with her class, waiting for me.

I have been worried for some time about the little garden we have in the quadrangle. It is the square in the middle of the building. We go all round it, on the inside, when we walk the corridor. Originally, it was paved, but apparently Mr Norman thought that it was boring and so he raised money from the parents to put plants in. He did it all by himself and lifted some of the pavers and planted shrubs in the soil. I am sure that it looked good when he finished it, but the groundsmen will not work in there. It is not on their schedule, so it is now overgrown, and nothing can be done about it. I told my friend, Cathy, and she immediately says that she will come to my rescue and offers to work in there, for free, after the garden centre closes on Wednesday.

"Don't say anything about payment," she emphasises, "because I want to do it for the children."

It is Wednesday evening now and our PTA meeting is crowded. Cathy arrives to do her work and apart from waving, I have no time to contact her.

"Right," James clears his throat, "let's make a start, we have lots to discuss. Firstly, I would like Miss Heron to explain the Community Aid Scheme. No need for minutes, this is an informal meeting." He does not look at me and keeps referring to his notes.

I go through the information as best I can. "We will be given money for the paint and materials to decorate the school, but we must provide the labour. The Governors agree if you are all willing to take part—"

"Right," interrupts James. "Let's have a vote then. Who is in favour?" Lots of hands go up.

"Against?" No hands. This is very good indeed, no one against, the scheme is going ahead.

"Good, now for the work rota, you can choose which room you want to decorate and when. We will be starting the first day of the holiday." Mrs Plane has drawn out a chart and soon the first week is filled with names. Mrs Feathers asks if she can organise an insurance 'just to be on the safe side'. Everyone agrees and she says she will get a quote and, after discussions with James, will put arrangements in place.

We talk about the final assembly next and our tribute to Mrs Dunn. We need it all to be secret, as a surprise for her, and our discussions are conducted with military precision. I am to present her with a watch which will be bought with the money donated by the parents. Sara offers to choose a little girl to present a bouquet. There are to be speeches from James and myself. We hope to have a photographer from our local paper. Mrs Jones is going to see if she can persuade the editor that he will sell hundreds more copies if a photo of Mrs Dunn's retirement presentation is on the front page!

"Thank you all for coming. Next term, when we meet, the school will look a lot brighter – just in time to welcome our new caretaker. The meeting is now closed." He catches my eye and gives a little nod with a smile. He gets up and taps his papers on the desk. Then he strides over to Paul Jones who runs a building and decorating business and will be particularly useful to us if he will help with our project.

Their conversation goes on for a long time and I take the opportunity to fill in some forms that need doing before the end of term. I wait until I hear the front door bang and the last of the parents must have left. I go round the school switching off the lights and I head through the front door and lock it. Suddenly, I hear light footsteps then a door slams and I see Sara's car disappear through the gate. It is then I notice that James' car is still there in the park. I can smell his tingling aftershave mingling with cigarette smoke.

"I thought the meeting went well, didn't you?" he is leaning against the wall and is shockingly near me. "I am looking forward to action, I don't like to spend too much time thinking about things." He stubs his cigarette out on the tarmac.

"What?" I am tired and my nerves are jangling a bit. Does he mean with me?

"The decorating I mean."

"Oh, oh, yes."

"Well, I must be off – Wendy will wonder where I've got to. We don't want her thinking I'm up to mischief now do we?" His car roars off and I go home.

Cathy rings.

"Hey, who was that handsome guy you were sitting next to?"

"Oh, you mean James?"

"You didn't tell me he was that good looking. I don't know how you can resist him."

"Oh, I hadn't noticed," I lie, and for some reason I think of that Headmistress losing her job over an affair. I need to be careful. I must resist him.

I hurriedly but profusely thank Cathy for her work and we arrange to meet up. She will still not take any money, but reluctantly agrees that I will pay when we next have a meal together.

For the few remaining weeks of term, I am busy with paperwork which keeps pouring in from County Hall. It seems that the fewer days there are left the more jobs there are. I work faster and faster until the last day when I must sign forms which I have not read because there is no more time.

July Sunday

Dear Dad,

I bet your blackberries are turning already – your cultivated fruits are always ready before the hedgerow ones. I am hoping that you will have some left by the time I get to your house next month. My little apple tree has had a good set – the frost must have missed the flowers, so I am hoping yours are the same.

Have you scythed the orchard yet? I remember trying to scythe when I came last year – I was hopeless and nearly cut my feet off at the ankles. It is a knack I never got – but I suppose that you have been using one all your life. 'Practice makes perfect', Mam used to say, but I gave up. You've always sworn by a scythe and how well it cuts. Even when you bought your lawnmower and the mechanical cutters arrived on the farm, you kept going with your own methods. It's paid off, because you would never get the lawnmower to cut through that rough grass in your orchard.

Do you remember my friend Cathy from Newford? Well, she's been to help with the little square garden at school. She has pruned all the bushes that had got completely out of hand and revealed a wooden seat in there. It all looks so clean and tidy now so the children will be able to use it again. I didn't dare let them in before in case it was dangerous with all the twigs and dead stuff on the concrete.

We are going to decorate the school ourselves and one of the fathers at school is a builder and he is going to order the paint for us. I am so pleased that he will be here. It seems such a big job and I will be glad of someone who knows what he is doing. His little boy is in the Infant class, and he is called Jason. He is a bright button and is already telling us all about undercoats and gloss paints. I know that the family have had a bit of trouble recently so I am hoping that this job will distract them.

We are getting ready for our end of term assembly – it is going to be a big event as we are saying 'Goodbye' to Mrs Dunn, our cleaner, and I want to do her proud.

I will let you know how I get on.

Love Vi xx

Chapter 18

The end of term assembly

I am quite nervous about the end of term assembly. This is the first one I have done, not only do we say goodbye to our two top juniors, but I must do Mrs Dunn proud.

I put our music on the record player. It has been chosen by Emily, it is 'The Waltz of the Flowers' and some children in my class are going to dance to it and the girls have adorned themselves with long dresses and drapes of their choice and are admiring each other. The boys of course did not want to dance.

Neville is in his element, though, putting the chairs out in the hall. He is busy making a gangway 'there could be a fire, right'. By mid-afternoon parents are pouring in and sitting on our little classroom chairs with their knees up to their chins. There are lots of toddlers too and they are getting restless running up and down Neville's gangway. He is busy adding to the confusion by chasing them.

Sara appears at the back of the hall with her little children lining up. All of them, including Sara, seem to have huge expectant eyes. My class is sitting at the side, they are trying to keep still but most of them fail, especially when they turn and recognise someone in the audience. They nudge each other and wave to their mums and dads. There is lots of whispering going on in this air of excitement.

James rushes in, smart and handsome as ever. And here is Mrs Dunn, still wearing her overall and short wellies. She has someone with her. Surely not? It can't be, can it? It is, it's Mr Norman, the last Head of the school who left me all that stuff to clear up. I wonder who invited him? Or did he invite himself? I am not sure that I am pleased to see him. I feel that I have been working in his shadow for all this time. Mrs Dunn is smiling at everyone but especially at Mr Norman, she is almost curtseying, as she bobs about trying to find a seat for him.

"Why, hello, Miss Heron, so nice to see you. So nice to be invited, I just could not let dear Mrs Dunn leave without saying farewell." This is Mr Norman greeting me as he adjusts his gold cufflinks and smooths his black blazer.

"Did I leave my fountain pen behind? Did you happen to find it? It doesn't matter if you can't put your hands on it at this particular moment, but I would like it back sometime. If that is not too much trouble." He smiles as he is speaking to me, but he is looking over his shoulder. He waves to Mrs Buckingham then catches Mrs Plane's eye and smiles. She smiles demurely and lowers her eyes.

Did he leave his fountain pen? He certainly did and a whole lot more besides! He probably left the kitchen sink too and I just have not been able to 'put my hands on it' yet.

I noticed Mrs Dunn rush off, whilst we were talking, and now she rushes back with one of her big black poly bags in tow. She almost disappears into it and then reappears with her newly permed hair sticking up in all directions.

"Here's your pen, Mr Norman. I kept it safe for you. I kept all the things you left." She bobs up and down in her eagerness to please. Mr Norman gives her a big hug. He takes his pen tucking it carefully into his lapel pocket but leaves the black bag deflated on the hall floor.

"You are wonderful – so wonderful, Mrs Dunn. I don't know how the school will manage without you."

Just then the press photographer arrives with cameras and flashguns around his neck. Mrs Jones has obviously done well with her powers of persuasion. Press photographers usually find better things, of more interest, at big schools in town.

At last, it is time for me to stand up and for the final assembly to begin. A hush of expectancy permeates the hall, everyone looks at me. I announce our first hymn and we all sing at the top of our voices, relieved to be getting going at last.

Caroline, in her little green uniform, goes over to the record player and puts our 'Waltz of the Flowers' music on again and the small group of girls move easily and unselfconsciously around the 'stage'. They have practised hours for these few minutes, but they have not wasted their time. Their steps match the notes and rhythm perfectly. We all clap.

"Beautiful," murmurs Mr Norman, just loud enough for us all to hear.

I ask the two children who are leaving to stand up and come to the front and both have prepared a little speech thanking the school and teachers and headteachers, 'especially Mr Norman and Miss Heron'. I give a short talk to wish them well in their new school, then it is time to say goodbye to Mrs Dunn.

I deliver my little speech, then ask James to give his vote of thanks. The vicar could not be here and has asked James to deputise for him. James has known Mrs Dunn for a long time. He speaks so eloquently with no notes and no hesitation. The history of Mrs Dunn's working life trips off his tongue. I listen in admiration of him, he occasionally catches my eye. The audience is not as attentive as me and some of them begin to shuffle.

When he finally finishes, I ask Mrs Dunn to come to the front for the presentation. She puts on a brave face as she pushes past people seated on the school chairs to get to me. I cannot help but feel sorry for her as she has always been so busy in school but now will have nothing to do. Everyone claps and, on cue, I see Sara at the back of the hall directing a little girl called Lucy down Neville's gangway.

But little Lucy, in her pretty pink dress, runs back and holds on to Sara. She has suddenly become 'all shy' and clingy. She will not come without Sara so they both walk forwards. We can all see huge tears brimming over Sara's cheeks as she helps to present the enormous bouquet. The audience is rivetted.

"Aah, aah."

"Isn't that lovely?"

"She's crying because Mrs Dunn is leaving."

"We'll all miss her."

Mrs Dunn stands in front holding her presents and beaming. She is still wearing her short wellies and overall, which look incongruous on this formal occasion. I wonder if she thinks that she is going to be called away any minute to unblock a lavatory. She launches uncertainly into a speech saying how much she has loved working for the kiddies and how the school just cannot be too clean and tidy for such precious little people.

Suddenly, Mrs Dunn's voice is drowned out by Sara's sobs which get louder and louder until she is totally overcome. Little Lucy, who is sitting on her knee, is being hugged tighter until she too bursts into tears. The children look on in bewilderment and awe while the mothers smile sympathetically.

Now, Mr Norman stands up and after a whispered conversation with the photographer he comes to the front. He beams out at us all as he adjusts his cufflinks once more.

I am standing at the side and James comes and stands next to me. I can smell his aftershave, it seems to be a different one, it is more spicey than before.

"Well, everyone, it is wonderful to see you all again." Mr Norman turns his head slowly surveying all the faces. "I am here to tell you all some good news. Mrs Dunn is going to help me in my big school in town."

"I don't think it is his school, he is only a senior teacher," whispers James leaning towards me so that his mouth tingles my ear.

"She is going to come and join our ladies' craft circle, to make things for the school. So, she will be very busy in her retirement won't she, children?"

"Yeeess," shout the children.

"Aren't we the lucky ones."

"Yeeess," echo the children again. The photographer has crept up Neville's gangway and is kneeling in front of her catching her attention.

"Look this way, Mrs Dunn."

Click, click, flash.

"Smile please."

Emily suddenly jumps up and runs down the corridor. She comes back with Mrs Dunn's court shoes from the caretaker's cupboard. Then, Mrs Dunn takes off her overalls to reveal her smart pale blue and white suit. She kicks off her wellingtons and giggles as she puts on her smart shoes, her transformation is complete. Mrs Dunn emerges like a flower from a bud. The children clap in delight and the parents smile.

Flash, flash, click.

"Now one with the little girl and the flowers."

"Just one more, could the dancers join you, Mrs Dunn?"

Sara puts on the music and, with a little persuasion after a short pause, Mrs Dunn slowly begins to sway to the dance music. We all clap out the rhythm.

As everyone leaves, I see that Mrs Plane is helping Mrs Dunn with the clearing, but I want a word. I ask her to come to the staffroom and she follows me quietly.

"Mr Plane, do you know who invited Mr Norman to our end of term assembly?" I ask. My voice is high pitched and tense.

"Oh, we always ask the last head to the end of term assembly," she says looking straight at me. She turns to go, then adds, "I invited him to save you the trouble – I thought that is what you would have wanted, and you would be pleased."

July Sunday

Dear Dad,

School has finished at last. I can hardly believe that I have been here two terms. I feel that I am really getting to know the children and am pleased with how the new maths and reading books are going down. It is a good sign that the parents want to help with the decorating of the school, it is a big task, but they seem so willing.

Our end of term assembly went well, and we said a sad farewell to Mrs Dunn, the cleaner, but she has volunteered to help at a school in Newford, so she will still be busy and using her talents in retirement.

We said 'Goodbye' to two of our older pupils, as well. They go on to the Comprehensive at Newford in September. I have only known them for two terms, but they are both doing well and will give Fish school a good reputation.

Mrs Field, our new cleaner, came to the assembly. She kept discretely in the background, but she was there smiling and clapping to support Mrs Dunn. Officially Mrs Field begins on 1st September, but I expect she will gradually take over in the holidays.

I took my friend, Cathy, out for her long overdue meal yesterday. And we went to that club that the young dustbin man told me about in Newford Community Hall. I was surprised that he remembered me and the school. He looked much happier than when I last saw him, he has taken up being a disc jockey full time. There was a bar and a cafe which did delicious meals.

I told Cathy about one of my blackcurrant plants that isn't doing well, she said that it was probably 'big bud' and I had to dig it out. So that is what I have done. I told Bill next door about it as well because he has some diseased blackcurrants. He has dug all his out and burnt them. He says he can't be bothered with fruit and vegetable growing, he has enough to do.

Are your onions ready for lifting yet? I remember last year they were early, and you dried them off in one of your old farm potato baskets. I hope that you have covered your carrots as the carrot fly is thriving this year.

My fish are doing well and are always hungry. They seem to be getting fatter by the minute. Mind you, I sometimes forget to feed them especially when I am busy at school or get back late. I am hoping that there are enough creatures in the pond for them to eat. *I will be interested to see how your fish are doing when I come.*

I bet your flower garden is a picture now with all your roses, marigolds, and sweet peas. I hope they hang on until I get there.

Love Vi xx

Chapter 19

Decorating

It is the first day of the summer holiday and now there is a long rest ahead. Pleasure seeps through me. I snuggle down under my bed covers until I remember that I should be decorating the school! Oh my God! I hastily jump out of bed and pull on an old tracksuit. Then I am off in a hurry and flurry before I have even had time for breakfast.

Today, we are painting the school courtesy of the CAS (Community Aid Scheme). I am trying to use letters, anyone who is anyone uses acronyms these days, but I usually forget what they mean.

There are already several cars in the car park at school when I arrive. Mrs Dunn must have unlocked the door. I go in to see that they are all at work. Paul Jones has set up some scaffolding and the upper walls have already been given a coat of paint.

How different it looks. All our reading books and new maths schemes are packed away in boxes and our workbenches and tables are pushed together and covered in sheets.

But who is that up on the scaffolding? I can hardly believe my eyes. Surely not? It is! It's Rebecca and she is up there wielding a paint brush. I stare disbelieving and open-mouthed, remembering all the times I have tried to get her to take part in PE. Even the sight of ropes and ladders for our lesson seemed to bring on a bout of Rebecca's illness or, worse still, an anguished meeting with her mother. But Rebecca is chatting and laughing with Mr Jones, on the top of the tower, seemingly without a care. Her legs stand solidly astride as she paints confidently and quickly. I search desperately for her mother. Who knows what trouble I will be in when Mrs Feathers sees where her sugar bag baby is now? At last, I see her and march urgently over to sort things out as quickly as I can before Rebecca does harm to herself.

"Have you seen what Rebecca is doing?" I try to sound calm. But Mrs Feathers looks unruffled as she glances towards Rebecca high above us.

"Oh yes, she loves working with Paul."

"But isn't all that physical exercise a bit worrying and then there's the height?"

"Oh no, this is different, this is fun and it's the holidays. It's not work, like PE in school. She is fine."

Ah well, I comfort myself, at least we have insurance.

Tim arrives carrying tins of paint for Sara's room and I follow him down the corridor.

"What colours has she chosen?" He lifts the lids and we eagerly peer in. One is rich terracotta, and the other is a deep leafy green. We both agree that this will make a beautiful combination. Trust Sara to go for trendy earthy colours. I admire her choice even though I have gone for something altogether more traditional. I remember my mother's advice was to always be on the safe side and so I chose magnolia.

Thinking about my room, I decide that I had better go and check what is happening there and see if there is anything I can do. James is sanding the walls and does not look up. In the kitchen Sara is hugging a mug of coffee. She is standing with a group of mums, wearing a fitted jumper which looks to be the exact shade of her terracotta paint. Her trousers are a deep green. I feel that I should be wearing magnolia.

I switch the kettle on.

"I'll do that, Vi. I'll make the helpers a drink. You have plenty to do organising things."

"Well, if you are sure, there is a dreadful noise in the hall. I think I had better investigate."

Back in the hall, I notice that there is an increasing number of unattended children racing about. This could be dangerous, and I begin to worry about accidents again.

"Children," I shout above the hubbub. I clap my hands and they all stop and look up at me.

"Children, please put your hands up if you came here on your own today." About half the hands go up.

"Now, those with their hands up must go straight home please. Come back when your parents are here."

The children left behind immediately get up and whizz around seemingly making more noise than before. Sara comes out with the tea tray which is seized upon by the grateful volunteers. Then Sara and I decide to occupy the children with games before there is an accident.

Things are going well on the decorating front; it is almost plain sailing.

The shift changes at lunchtime and James leaves without even saying goodbye to me. Sara must go, and Tim has already left.

Mrs Weatherall is the leader of the next working group.

"Right then, we're ready, Miss 'eron, what do you want us to do?"

I give instructions.

"Right you are, leave it to us. Come on, everybody, let's get going." She beckons and marshals her little group of helpers. Off they go to work without a backward glance. She seems full of enthusiasm as she commands her troops. But they have not been gone long before she is back standing in front of me with a cigarette lolling at the side of her mouth and her arms tightly folded over her apron.

"I can't do nothing with 'em."

"What do you mean, Mrs Weatherall?"

"When I told 'em what to do some of 'em got nasty. I said to do the gloss and they want to do the emulsion."

155

"Let's go and see." I am using delaying tactics again, hoping for things to calm down, and waiting for inspiration on how to solve the dispute.

"Look!" Mrs Weatherall stands, hands on hips, while the ladies have their backs to her. They are determinedly painting emulsion on the walls with rollers.

Paul Jones is standing nearby and shouts, "The lad will do all the gloss on the windows, won't you, lad?" I had not realised that he had brought a helper. The lad sniffs and comes over with his pot of gloss and starts on the windows immediately. Mrs Weatherall stands for a minute then shrugs before getting going on the emulsion with vigour.

We agreed to have Sunday off, so I have a rest in the morning and in the afternoon, I pop round to see Joyce and Bill for a bit of company. The warmth of their house wafts over me as I go through their front door. The central heating is full on even though it is summer.

Joyce and Bill are arguing again about money this time. Joyce wants new curtains, like mine, 'they would make the house warmer'. Warmer? Surely the house would go into spontaneous combustion if it got any hotter. Bill is having none of it and buries his head in his Sunday newspaper.

"I want my house to look smart like yours," she confides. We stare round at her floral patterns, then she sighs and seems to give up. I am surprised she thinks mine is 'smart'. I suppose she means that there is hardly any furniture. There is not much there to make it look untidy.

"I am still so sorry about letting you down about the cleaning job. But Bill says it's all for the best because he doesn't think I would ever get to grips with the heating system."

"Oh, that's all over and done with now." We smile and gradually, with the television droning on and the heat from the fire, we all nod off. The next thing I hear is Joyce's voice saying that tea is ready. I had not meant to stay that long, but she has already opened a tin of salmon especially for me.

When I finally get home, I go straight upstairs because my 'smart' house is cold and I just cannot resist my cosy bed.

Monday and Tuesday go well at school and the volunteers get on quickly with the work. But on Wednesday there is no one at the school. I carry on painting Sara's room on my own. The colours look good and when she puts her plants back in it will all look like a woodland for the children. I hear the front door bang, 'Oh good, help at last'. But it is only Neville.

"Can I 'elp out a bit, Miss 'eron? I'm good at painting, right."

"Yes, alright, but be careful." I grudgingly allow him, as no one else is here to help. He whoops off into the hall and has a bounce on the squashy mat. A small gang of parents eventually arrives. Someone switches on a portable radio and, with music blaring, they trot off to the kitchen to make tea. Paul Jones arrives in the afternoon, but this is his last day. He cannot afford to take more time off work. I am beginning to worry about getting the job done.

By Friday it is clear that we can't possibly do the work; the volunteers have dried up. What on earth will I do? I am here on my own again. I wander around dispirited, kicking aimlessly at the dustsheets and staring at the endless paint brushes and half painted sticks which have been used for stirring, some of them look suspiciously like my school pencils.

The front door bangs and this time I do not even bother to look up. If it is Neville, he is out of luck today, I cannot tolerate him messing around. But it is not Neville it is James. He charges in and surveys the scene with his cigarette clenched between his teeth, swivelling around on his heels. An army of helpers follows him in quick succession. There is Sara (in red dungarees), Beth, Tim, Mrs Plane, and a whole group of determined looking parents. James commands everyone and they all scurry to get on with their jobs. Even Darren, Neville's big brother, turns up and starts painting the staffroom walls. It is not long, though, before he is puffing and panting and red in the face. He slows to a stop.

157

"It's blinking 'ard work Miss 'eron, our Neville never told me it was like this. I just came to play on the mat." He wipes his sweating forehead on his sleeve. "Neville said you'd 'ave drinks and all that." I take him to the kitchen, and he helps himself to biscuits and some orange squash.

"It's still a bit funny that you're a 'eron and 'eron eat fish and Fish is where we live. I worked that out myself. Do you get it?"

"Yes, I know what you mean. I thought of that too when I first came. But don't worry, Darren, Fish village is too big for me to swallow. So, you are all quite safe."

"Yes, but Fish might swallow you. Mr Norman told us about a chap in the Bible who was swallowed by a whale. So, watch out."

"Yes, I think I had better be careful, thank you for the warning." I smile, but Darren's face shows me that he is in earnest.

"But I wouldn't worry if I was you because the big fish sicked up that old man. So, you'll be alright in the end."

The volunteers gradually disappear during the day and eventually there is only me with Sara and James. We sit and have a cup of tea.

"We soon got that done," says James.

"Yes, it must have taken inches off my rear," says Sara wiping her soft brown hair from her face. She has a tiny smudge of paint on her nose. James studies her and smiles but says nothing.

"There is still the staffroom to finish off, and part of my classroom, and then all the clearing." I survey the paint pots and sheets and unwashed brushes.

"Well, I am off on holiday tomorrow, got to go and help Wendy with the packing. We need an early start to get to the Isles of Scilly. The traffic around Okehampton can be bumper to bumper if you are late."

"Oh, how wonderful," gushes Sara, pushing away another stray strand of hair and smiling at James.

"Well, I will lock up and be in touch with you, James, say a week before the end of the holiday." I try to sound convincing, but I am beginning to wonder if we have been foolish thinking that we could decorate a school. Sara leaves and then James follows immediately afterwards. I wash the cups and finally lock the door, turning my back on the disarray and trying not to be too dismayed. I wonder if the County Offices have a help team for schools using this scheme. I should have thought of this before. I should have asked.

August Sunday

Dear Dad,

We are getting on very well with the decorating at school. Everyone is so good hearted, and the rooms are looking very clean and fresh with their new coat of paint. One good thing is that because we are decorating, County Hall sent someone out to repair our roof, at last. Anyway, it is waterproof now! They came with roofing material and heated up a big vat of tar and went to work. So, all is well for now on that score. They also replaced some panels which had come off the hall roof before I came here, and they repaired the damage to the plaster on the inside walls. I am very relieved all that has been done, at last.

Are you still getting moles digging up your lawn? I remember them last year and I think that the smoke 'bombs' helped so we could try those again this year if you want.

I am not feeding the birds this summer; I think that there is so much natural food, including weeds, in my garden so that they will easily find stuff to eat. I miss watching them though. I bet your bird table is full of your birds of paradise especially if the young have fledged.

I am looking forward to coming to see you again.

Love Vi xx

Chapter 20

Summer holiday

After a week of doing nothing very much, I set off to Dad's. I had intended to do lots of jobs around the house and sort the garden once and for all, but I was tired after the decorating at school and decided to catch up when I got back. I rested and read and chatted to Joyce over the garden fence. Finally, I packed my case and went.

The journey is enjoyable this time as I settle to an easy speed and stop off twice. Finally, I roll into Dad's drive. I let myself in and smell that unmistakable whiff of tobacco smoke.

For a moment he is not aware of me. I watch him lying on his settee perfectly still with his hands on his lap. He is staring unblinking at the wall. His pipe is on the little plastic table next to him with all the dirty smoking paraphernalia; lighter, matches in case of failure, various prodders and his Condor baccy spilling out.

"Hello, Dad, I'm here at last," I shout, putting down my hastily packed case. His head suddenly swivels, and his clouded blue eyes hardly seem to know who I am. Recognition dawns slowly.

"You made me jump. I didn't hear your car." His face changes immediately as he jumps up to put the kettle on. The mugs are already set out in the kitchen and the teapot has a new, but now soggy, teabag in. The long-life milk he has started to use, because the pasteurised went 'off', gives a distinctive aroma. We sit down and drink in silence. Dad on his settee and me on the pink chair covered by my mother years ago.

"Aye well, I'd better be getting on." He stands up wearily and goes outside. He seems smaller and his hair thinner and greyer. His baggy grey trousers are held up by braces over his shirt with rolled-up sleeves.

We spend a few days, with Dad in his garden, and me cleaning and cooking and shopping. A bit of telly at night with Dad falling asleep to complete the day's unbreakable routine.

"Why don't you come back with me, Dad?"

"What for?"

"For a bit of a holiday – a change."

"I can't leave your mam. And we haven't got that headstone yet."

"Well, let's go to the stonemasons today and see how they are getting on, first." So that is what we did. The headstone was ready, and they would put it up when we were away. The wording was at the top 'Much loved wife, mother, grandmother...' the writing stopped halfway down, and I knew, with a sudden awful ache, that it was waiting for my father to die when his inscription could be added.

"I'll have to tell your mam." He packed a spade and some rusty sheep clippers, with the big flat criss-cross blades, used for shearing wool off sheep's backs, so many years ago. I can remember him doing the job with deft strong hands, his body melding with that of the sheep as he bent over it. It would be a concentrated session and he would not look up until the wool was on the ground and the sheep bare and shivering, before it dazedly ran away.

At the last minute he rushed into the garden and picked a bunch of flowers. Gaudy red and yellow dahlias the size of saucers. My mother liked subtle flower colours, green suffusing into white. He returned to the house and came back with a Kilner jar.

We went to the grave. He tidied it up, dug round, flattened some clods, and cut some tufts of grass with his sheep shears. Then it was to the water butt with the jar. Finally, the flowers, already lolling their heads, were placed carefully in the water.

The arrangement went on the hump of grass that was now my mother. Dad and I stood silently then he spoke gently.

"Ta-ra, love, I'm off to Vi's for a day or two, won't be long." He took his trilby hat off and bowed his head for a few seconds and then we were off, in a big hurry, back to my car.

We set off to my house, after Dad packed a case. It used to be my mother's, bought for her hospital stays. It is blue, her favourite colour, kept under the bed. Dad secures it with an old leather belt (it looks suspiciously like part of a horse's bridle from long ago). He says that it is so that 'nothing spills out'. But nothing would spill out, there is hardly anything in it, just a spare pair of underpants, a shirt and at my persuasion a spare pair of trousers. There is a comb and a tube of Steradent tablets. Dad puts his best sports jacket on and his trilby hat, of course, then we are on our way.

We head through Hull passing the docks and then straight on with the Humber on our left. Dad says nothing but looks out of the window with his head away from me. Then we are on the motorway which was a new thing for him. I do not think that he had been on one before, at least not for any distance. We head across England on the M62.

"So that's what the hard shoulder means, I always wondered." He thought it was a waste of money having so much tarmac not being used. We pass a sign saying, 'The North, the South'.

"They want to make up their minds – it can't be both." I explain that we are going west and that you can only come off left from the motorway so...

"So that road will branch... good idea. One road north and one road south, probably onto the Great North Road." He quickly understands.

"We use the M1 instead, though it follows the same direction. You've been on the Great North Road, haven't you, Dad?"

"Aye, it goes from London to Edinburgh. It was a grand road. Sid and me went to Scotland and bought those sheep. They were cheap, by gum they were. But they were no good, you know."

"Why not?"

"Well, they kept on getting out. They were used to roaming where they wanted and didn't like being penned in. I got rid of them in the end."

As we swoop along, he follows all the towns and cities on the signs. He asks me where to next, then breathes a sigh of relief when we arrive. It is as if by willing the town to come in sight he has achieved a purpose when we get there, or at least when we bypass it.

We arrive at Wenbrook, then number 10 and we stop in the drive. Dad jumps out and runs straight through to the back. I am wondering how he will feel in this rather built-up hilly village when he is used to his own quieter little place with flat land all around. But his only comment is about my garden.

"Your garden's a mess. Your other blackcurrants have big bud as well. I'll have to sort you out." And that is what he did all week. With his shirt sleeves rolled up and his trilby hat on, he dug all the vegetable patch with lines that were straight and clean as if a plough had gone through. He treated the lawn for moss and cut it and edged it. He trimmed and pruned all my bushes. He never stopped from dawn to dusk. I felt so bad about the blackcurrants. He wanted me to have them, and I had let him down. He dug them out without a word of reproach. After a week I took him back.

"*Home James and don't spare the horses,*" he shouted as soon as we were on our way. The name 'James' startled me for a moment. 'How does he know James?' I wondered until I quickly realised that he was quoting an old song he knew. He began to sing "*I'm ruined as ruined can be...*"

We arrive at his home in record time, he did not want to stop on the way back. He rushes into his garden before unlocking the front door.

"The cabbages are a mess. There's caterpillars all over them. I'd better get on with spraying." And that is what he does, while I unpack his case and do some washing. As I was hanging his clothes in the wardrobe, I noticed that my mother's clothes had been tidied, but they hung lifeless and somehow pathetic, after all these months. My mother was always a smart dresser and her clothes always fitted perfectly but these looked like shapeless, colourless bags.

"I've been thinking," says Dad that night. "I'm sure that your idea of a computer is a good thing. Your children at Fish should not be backward. Just because they are village children you don't want to be behind the times." With that he brings his cheque book and sits down at the table. He signs his name on a blank cheque.

"Here," he says.

"How much are you giving?"

"Ten pounds."

"I'll write it now." I say, "Ten pounds only."

He gets up and goes to lie in his favourite place on the settee.

"Thank you, Dad, that is so kind."

"Not kind, but I believe in being one step ahead, like I had to be on the farm when I was buying and selling. I didn't make many mistakes except for them sheep from Scotland."

"That is really kind of you..."

"That's done and I don't want to hear any more about it." He settles down to watch the news. "The swallows are feeding their babies in my garage, you know."

"I have seen them, Dad, swooping in and out through the open window."

I leave the next day, Dad is in his garden busily weeding and spraying.

August Sunday

Dear Dad,

I have just got home, and I know that I have only just left you, but I thought that you would still like a letter to arrive on Wednesday. My garden looks so tidy after all your work – thank you very much, it is a very good job done. I am sorry about the blackcurrants and thank you for offering to buy me some more. This time I won't let you down.

I am going back into school tomorrow, we have almost finished our decorating, but I need to check that we are all ready for the new term. I am looking froward to seeing the rooms again, painted, and fresh. Everyone in the village seems to have had a hand in the decorating, I think villages are like that aren't they? Not like a big town where no one knows their neighbours.

It was good that you met Joyce and Bill. It was nice of them to ask us round for a cup of tea. I thought that they would, they have become good friends to me. They wished that they were good gardeners like you. I am afraid that they do not bother much except Bill cuts the lawn. They argue about it a lot, but it is only good-humoured banter. Joyce puts annuals in the front, and you saw that it is a riot of colour now. It was a good thing that they got rid of their blackcurrants as soon as they knew about the big bud. Bill apologised for his plants infecting mine with the mite.

Your gladioli looked stunning, Dad, I love the bright red and yellows shining out into the summer sun.

Love Vi xx

And now I am back in school. I am alone with a mass of paint pots and dirty brushes that we all forgot to clean before we left. There is still the staffroom to finish and some gloss on the skirting boards. Then, of course, we must clear. I say 'we' but at this rate it will be just me and we are in the last week of the holidays. I left a message on James' phone but there has been no reply. I wonder how ever I will manage to get everything ready for the new term.

"Hello," I hear a voice as the front door slams. I recognise the heavy breathing; it is Miss Nelson the Headteacher at Bridlypool. It seems a long time since we were at the swimming lesson.

"I saw your car and wondered how you were getting on. Oh, my goodness what a mess!"

"We were doing so well at the beginning of the holiday, but I am on my own now." Miss Nelson rushes out and I hear her car door open. That is that then, she will have no patience with me doing a job that should, by rights, have been done by County Hall. But then the school door bangs, and I hear Miss Nelson's heavy breathing once more. She appears in the doorway dressed in her white gym shoes and a huge dark green waterproof apron. She rolls her sleeves up.

"Right, what do you want me to do?" I am shocked into silence; I never expected her help only recriminations for being so stupid. We work together all day; I share my sandwiches with her. We finish the painting and throw the old pots and dirty brushes in the dustbins outside. At the end of the day, we also finish the remains of the whisky.

"I have handed in my resignation, my dear, with effect from the end of this year. I've had enough, it's time for the younger ones, like you, to take over now." I want to say something kind and clever but we both nod off. We wake up feeling cold and stiff.

Chapter 21

Autumn term

I decided to buy some new clothes before the start of school. I have been struggling along with my interview outfit and a few summer dresses. Cathy came with me, but she was not interested in buying clothes, at least, not the sort I was buying. I wanted up-to-date smart professional outfits. We went to Debenhams and Richards shops but, when I had finished, she popped into a charity shop. It was Oxfam and she bought a warm jacket for work and a scarf. Then we went back to her house and chatted, sitting round her fire with a glass of organic wine each.

The new term has begun, my third term, here at Fish school and everything seems new and fresh. I draft a letter immediately to thank the parents for all their work. But it is not just that the school has been painted. We have a new cleaner, Mrs Field, who meets me at the door with her duster in hand and her earrings shining as bright as her smile. I have new children in my class, two from Sara's Infants. Sara has one new child, just coming up to her fifth birthday.

At the weekend, I did something I have been meaning to do for at least a term. I have bought a hamster for my class. I went into Newford to the big pet shop there. It is a lovely golden creature and seems to sleep for most of the day. I bought a second-hand cage that I saw in Oxfam. I wanted to get a small creature for the children to look after but, so far, I have not had time to even think about it.

A little boy called Eric Edwards has moved up to my class. He seems so small, if I did not know his date of birth, I would think that there was some mistake and that he should still be an infant. He loves the hamster and cannot take his eyes off it.

There is also Aurora, who should be here in my class now, having moved up from Sara's class. She is a traveller and lives in a caravan in the field next to the school, she must have some arrangement with Peter's parents, I think. In any case, it is gone nine o'clock and she is not in school. Perhaps she is ill but, after all, she only lives a field away, it would not take her mother long to get here and let me know.

I have no time to worry about that, though, all the children are sitting here (apart from Aurora) looking scrubbed and expectant for the autumn term when they can make a fresh start and do well. There are new coats to be hung up and recently bought pencil cases to get used to and lots of catching up to do with friends who live on distant farms.

We make a start, after Mrs Plane's dinner money collection, with writing about what we have done in the summer holidays. It is not very original, but the children do not know that, and settle eagerly to write about what they have been doing.

It is just then that Aurora runs in through the side door followed by her mum. Neither of them has a jacket and Aurora's cardigan is tied round her waist.

"I am so sorry to be late, Miss Heron. We didn't wake up till nine and then it was such a rush to get Aurora ready for school. I'll do better tomorrow. I promise." And with that she smiles an apology and disappears.

Suddenly, I hear the front door bang. Who can this be now? I have just settled the children after the interruption with Aurora. It is James.

"Hi, all present and ship-shape?" He holds his cigarette behind his back away from the children. "Good job done with the decorating. It is all looking very professional and clean."

He does not mention the bits of wall that had been left to paint, nor the clearing up I had to do with Miss Nelson.

"I've been asked to go to County Hall to talk to the officials about the CAS scheme and how it worked so well here. On my way..." Before I have time to answer and tell him that it did not work that well for me, he salutes and rushes off. I hear the door bang.

It is then I smell that unmistakable smell of urine. I walk around the classroom in the general direction of the distinctive aroma. It is coming from Eric. I leave the children busy with their work and go down the corridor to Sara's class.

"Oh, I've been meaning to talk to you about little Eric for ages. Mr Norman and I thought he would grow out of it."

"Well, he hasn't, I must see his parents about it."

"They are lovely, and they have tried everything and have been very worried. I have been changing him every day." She rushes off to her cupboard and brings back a spare pair of underpants and elasticated trousers.

"Would it be best if I changed him – do you think, Vi? He is used to me." We agreed, so that is what she did. I think I had better strike while the iron is hot, so to speak, and I decide to go and see Eric's parents tonight. He usually walks home so I will take him home in my car. I want to talk to his mum and dad, face to face, and see what can be done.

"Now, Eric, I want you to tell me how to get to your home," I use a gentle voice so as not to frighten him. We follow the main road through the village.

"Down there," says Eric suddenly. I back up and go down a lane with grass and moss growing in the middle. It got bumpy.

"Are you sure this is the way?"

"Yes."

"There's my house." Eric points to a building, down an even narrower track. My car breathes in as it bumps and scrapes to the house.

There are ducks paddling in a stream and I wonder if one of these had been snatched for our raffle prize. The hens scatter at the sight of my car. I get out and take in the breath-taking view. The little cottage stands on the side of a wooded valley with larch trees crowding over protectively. I can make out a river running away into the darkness of the valley bottom. A pig snorts and heaves his front feet up on the pigsty half-door. Eric had long since disappeared.

I tiptoe through the muck and knock on the door.

"Hello," I shout, "it's Miss Heron, from the school."

"Madge," a man's voice calls from the pigsty and eventually a heavily pregnant woman comes scurrying.

"Come in, Miss Heron, I'm sorry I didn't hear your car." We sit down staring at the fire which does not seem to give out any heat in this gloomy, dark room.

"Will you have a cup of tea?"

"No thank you, I have to get back to school to do some more work. I came to see you about Eric."

Mrs Edwards sits on the edge of her chair staring intently at the fire and ringing her hands.

"Oh, Miss Heron, I am at my wits' end with him. I just don't know what else to do." It is as if a dam of pent-up words has broken free, as she tells me about the wet sheets and all his wet clothes and about the problems of washing and drying especially now the summer is over. "His dad has tried every punishment – but nothing works."

"Well, I would like to try and get help for Eric. I need your permission to call the Educational Psychologist to make an assessment." I try to sound matter of fact and gentle. I do not want to frighten her off.

"I am sure that won't be necessary, Miss Heron. Mr Norman said that he would grow out of it, and I am sure that he is right."

"It hasn't gone away though, has it?"

"You are young and modern, Miss Heron – Mr Norman understood – but if you want to help, perhaps you could contact the School Nurse for us, she may be able to find someone to help with all the washing."

She is following a pattern I have seen before, trying to cope with a problem rather than tackling the reasons for the difficulties.

"Think about it, Mrs Edwards, and I will be in touch again. Talk with your husband and see what he thinks too." I leave without much hope and get back to school to finish my marking.

The following week we start preparing for Harvest Festival, it will be an especially important time for this farming community. Sara tells me that they all go up the hill to the church and the vicar holds a service of thanksgiving.

"Do they bring harvest gifts?" I ask.

"Some do, but Mr Norman left it to the vicar really."

I talk to my class about the service. As usual they are full of ideas.

"We can bring things to give to old people from our gardens – like fruit and flowers," says Emily. They want to write poems and draw pictures to cheer lonely people.

"What about inviting people to the service, you know, those who live alone," suggests Caroline.

I ring the vicar to ask if he will come in to discuss the festival with me. Just as I put the phone down it rings a gain. It is Mr Edwards.

"I hear you want our Eric to see a shrink."

"Well, that is not quite how I would describe it, but the Educational Psychologist might be able to shed some light on how we can help Eric overcome his problem."

"I don't see a problem that could not be sorted by a quick kick up the backside. But we are at our wits' end and so you can have a try with your educational bod – so long as he gets some action fast. The wife is due to give birth soon and I can't have her worried to death."

I did not make promises because in my experience it takes a long time to sort this sort of thing; it is not usually caused by one problem. The vicar arrives.

"I would like the service to be in school this year if you agree. You would be in charge at the event, of course."

"It is a thanksgiving to God and should be held in a place of worship. These children are my parishioners and part of my flock."

"Yes, I understand that, but could you conduct the service in school?"

"I would like my homage to God to be in our much loved and holy church."

"I think that a service in school would mean a great deal to the children. They could become more involved by devising their own thanks."

"Your previous incumbent cast no such doubt on our place of worship nor our order of service. It is one of the highlights of the Church's year. However, I will consider what you have said in depth, and pray to God for an answer."

I will have to put my plans on hold for now, it would not be fair to take it any further with the children only for them to be disappointed.

Mr and Mrs Edwards arrive unannounced at the end of the school day. I usher them into the staffroom and little Eric squeezes in at the last minute. He sits on the edge of the chair swinging his legs.

"Right, I'll come straight to the point. As you know, I've decided that he will see this psychological man of yours. Madge needs help, what with the babby being due any minute." Who said that the Ed Psych was a man? I know, of course, that it is a man, so I do not say anything.

"How does it work?"

"Someone will come to talk to you and then they will see Eric, separately. Do you understand that, Eric?" I ask. He swings his legs harder and nods.

"Speak up," bellows his dad. "We can't hear you."

"Yes," whispers Eric.

"There will be an assessment and then a report and a plan of action."

"How soon?"

"It is in the hands of the Psychological Service, but I hope that it will not be too long. I will keep you informed at each stage."

"I don't want anybody knowing about this, you understand?"

"Of course, it is all entirely confidential."

"That's that then," he stands up and Madge heaves herself off the chair. Little Eric bolts as they both leave.

"I'll be in touch," I shout to their retreating backs. Madge turns to smile.

A week later the Educational Psychologist arrives, by appointment, to see Eric and his parents. He is a tall amiable looking man wearing a very smart suit and carrying a black leather briefcase.

"Hi, call me Andy. Now, who am I here to see today?" I settle him at my desk and go to get a cowering Eric. He is wet. I take him to the toilets to help him change quickly and go with him to see the Ed Psych. Eric creeps in and sits down on the edge of a chair again with his hands on the seat taking some of his meagre weight. He licks his lips and looks as if he is about to make a bolt for it at any minute.

His parents arrive at the front door, and I rush to greet them. Madge is wearing a huge tent-like dress with a big white collar and Mr Edwards has a tweed jacket on, with smart trousers. His hair is slicked back with what looks like Brylcreem. His face is bright red. He pulls uneasily at his collar. "Are we all in here? Ah, there you are, Eric, I hope you're going to speak up this time."

"Now, Eric, there is no need to be afraid. I am Mr Phillips and am here to meet you and then have a little chat with your parents. I will talk to you when I come again in school time. If you could wait in your classroom..." Eric licks his sore lips and scarpers. I close the door on his parents and the Ed Psych and hope for miracles. Eric is in my classroom again playing with the hamster.

The next day, Caroline's mum is waiting for me early in the morning, she looks so neat and tidy just like Caroline always does. She puts me to shame.

"I am worried about Caroline and the hamster, Miss Heron."

"Why, he is so dopey and gentle with the children, he is mostly sleepy because he is a nocturnal animal. He will not hurt her. Caroline seems very fond of him, as do all the children."

"It's not that. It's, well – I don't know how to say this."

"What is it? What seems to be the problem, Mrs Dove?"

"Well, what about his wee and poo?"

"No one seems to have got dirty so far, they are very clean creatures. Look." She glances sideways at the cage but still looks doubtful. Then she hands me a package that she has been holding on to for grim death during our discussion. I open the brown bag and inside is an apron and some rubber gloves.

"Just in case."

"Yes, of course. We will keep these near the cage for Caroline to use."

But she does not seem reassured and stands there looking down wringing her hands. The children are beginning to tumble in and so I walk with her through to the kitchen. Beth takes one look and puts the kettle on. I smile gratefully and dash back to my class.

At play time I pop in to thank Beth.

"Oh, she has had such a rough time. She lost two babies before Caroline came along," sighs Beth. "Two baby boys, one miscarried and one was still-born."

"Poor Mrs Dove, I had no idea, no wonder she is trying to keep safe by being clean all the time. I don't know how to help."

"None of us do, Miss Heron, we help by listening, I think. That's all we can do."

September Sunday

Dear Dad,

Before I write any more, I want to thank you again, for the money towards our school computer. Rebecca's mum started the fund and another of our parents has had a try but neither of them did very well. Mr Shawell, one of our Governors, has taken it over now. He has set up a bank account, so I will be able to add your money when I next see him.

I was surprised when he came to see me because he seemed too upper crust for the village, and I thought that he was not very bothered about the school. But I must have been wrong because he told me that he often travels to his business in London, and he has been told by the director that computers are going to be the tool of the future. So, he is keen that we have one at Fish. I know you don't want me to give anymore thanks, I will say no more except to say that I'll let you know how we get on. Now Mr Shawell is working with us I think we will manage very well.

The school looked ready for the new term after all our efforts. I know that you say a ten-year-old school should not need decorating, but it was in a bad state. I can't help but think that we have a fantastic set of parents who will give their time like that.

I went off to a farm in the hills the other week. You should have seen it – so ancient it was like going back 30 years – to when I was a little girl on our farm. They had a pig which surprised me as you do not usually see pigs here on the land. It is mostly sheep and milking herds of cows.

I have been to the clothes shops, at last, and bought some more smart clothes. I have chosen some blouses with big silk bow ties like Maggie Thatcher wears. I bought a dress, like hers too, with a blue neck ribbon. The skirts I chose are a bit shorter and tighter than Maggie's, but I think that they suit me. I didn't spend as much as I really need to on clothes, though, because I am still saving for a new car. My old one is not reliable, and I can't afford for it to break down in the winter, especially if it is a bad one like last year.

You will be picking the last of your beans and peas I should think – they have done so well this year. It's probably about the time you start clearing up in the garden and digging over the veg

177

*plot, but your Michaelmas daisies should be out and your dahlias
even bigger and better than when I was with you.*

Love Vi xx

Chapter 22

Harvest Festival

It is Thursday night; I am having a rest, after a busy day at school, when my phone rings.

"Hello, Vi."

"Hello. Dad, are you alright?"

"Yes, I've been thinking."

"What about?"

"Well, it's all these vegetables and soft fruit I have. I told you there's far too many for me, now I am on my own. I think I'll start pickling and bottling some of them. Your mam used to do that; you know."

"It's a good idea, Dad. I remember Mam doing that. She used Kilner jars like the one you took to the grave."

"Aye, I've still got all her jars. I've sorted them out from the garage. I saw that the swallows had fledged when I was in there. They will soon be on their way to Africa. I don't know how they do it, but it all works out for them in the end – life is like that with nature."

"Do you know how to pickle, Dad?"
"Well, I've searched out your mam's WI recipe book and it tells you in there."

"I'll look forward to seeing what you have done when I come at half-term."

"Another thing I've been thinking about is that farm you went to up in the hills. You said that you have herds of cattle, your way. Do you remember when ours got the staggers?"

"Yes, it was such a worry when they all started getting ill."

"Well, we had the Vitinary worried, he tried everything and then we hit on the answer."

"Wasn't it the old paint on the gates?"

179

"Yes, they were licking it and it had lead in. Who would have thought that? They got lead poisoning and were staggering everywhere. Vitinary had never heard of it before. The answer isn't always simple in life, you know. But there is an answer."

At school, we are all excited about doing our own Harvest Festival. The vicar has kindly agreed that we have two festivals, one in school and one in church.

Caroline has taken charge. She has made a list of all the gifts the children are going to bring. We have talked about what would be suitable. Emily wants the vegetables to go to old people who cannot grow their own. She too is making a list.

"Marrows are not really a good idea; can you think why?" I ask, trying to get them to think about what people would do with them.

"If it was a big marrow, right, they wouldn't be able to carry it," quips Neville. "Old people are not very strong."

"And what about windfall apples?"

"No good," says Peter, "they are already beginning to rot. Better to bring handpicked fruit." He knows all about country matters from his farm and the children seem impressed as they do not question him further.

I worked out an order of service with the vicar and sent a letter to the parents. I am looking forward to the event, well, to both events.

When I arrive at school, on the great day, there is a new car in the car park, it is a sporty Jag. A very smart man steps out. He is trimmer and even smarter than James and it takes me some time before I realise that it is Mr Hall, the adviser, who interviewed me for this job from County Hall. I wish he had let me know he was arriving; I feel so unprepared, on the hop, so to speak.

Mr Hall springs across the car park, holding out his hand, with a broad smile on his face and his dark eyes, as piercing as they were on my interview.

"I have to be in this area, Vi, so I thought that I'd pop in and see how you are getting on. I am sorry that I have not been sooner, but you are so isolated here it is difficult to fit in a visit."

"I am pleased that you have come," I say hoping to sound sincere.

"Well, I can be with you all morning, so we will have a good catch up. Just carry on as if I were not here." Easier said than done. I had hoped to spend the morning sorting out the Harvest Festival at a leisurely pace, but that was not possible now. I wanted to show Mr Hall how I was managing in the school, but this was not a good time. I soldier on trying to keep the children in a quiet routine.

Once we are underway, the adviser goes to sit with one group doing their maths. Suddenly, Neville begins to crack silly little jokes. Normally, no one takes any notice, but the new visitor has made us all a bit tense, and some children start to think Neville is amusing. I go and sit at his table and quieten him down whilst keeping an eye on Mr Hall who eventually saunters off down the corridor to Miss Faye's classroom.

Mr Hall has decided to stay for lunch. I wish he would just leave, and think again that this is not a good time for me to have an inspection about how well I am settling in. Thankfully, the children begin their dinner time without a fuss. I sit down with Mr Hall at the staff table. Beth comes out to greet him like a long-lost friend. Mrs Plane creeps in like an apparition in her long fawn cardigan. She is seated before I even hear her footsteps. Sara bounces in favouring Mr Hall with her beautiful smile.

He charms us all, asking Mrs Plane about her husband's farm and Miss Faye about her flat. He asks me if I have met any of my colleagues in neighbouring schools. He listens encouragingly to us all as if fascinated by our answers. He discusses the price of sheep; the wonderful earth colours Sara has chosen for her room and the possibility of a new colleague for me, at the school nearby, now Miss Nelson is leaving.

Suddenly, Jake comes up to the staff table. The children are not supposed to do this.

"My mum bought me a new book, yesterday." Sara puts her arm round him and Mr Hall smiles and nods. Jake seems to recognise him and smiles and nods back.

"It's a lovely book, Jake. An expensive hardback book. Come along now, let's go to your table," says Sara calmly.

"Oh, it's not just a hard back," answers Jake, not moving, "it's got a hard front as well." All of us smile at his literal understanding of 'hardback'. Jake smiles confidently and then turns to go with Sara.

The end of dinner bell is rung, and Mr Hall gets up. The children come puffing in with their usual singsong, 'Sin time', meaning that it is time to come in.

"Well, I must be going, Vi, keep up the good work, I can see you have settled in." Just then Neville comes blustering up to me with a brown paper bag of potatoes.

"I've just remembered these, right. I'd left them in the cloakroom. I dug them up this morning, right, they are bastards from last year – a bit mucky, but they make good chips, right."

"You know where all the other harvest produce is, Neville, can you put them there... before..."

I am too late the bag has burst and the potatoes and mud drop onto the polished wooden floor next to Mr Hall's immaculate shoes. He rushes to the door.

"I'll leave you to it."

"What did you think of my new maths scheme, the new reading books and the decorating...?" He cannot hear me, but he waves cheerily as he strides off to his Jag. He zooms away at top speed; his sports car looks incongruous as a tractor edges past. I had hoped for more praise but, never mind, I have the all-important Harvest Festival to think of.

Neville prepares the hall again, with his central aisle or 'gangway' as he calls it. Caroline and Peter put all the gifts carefully on our temporary stage. There is so much produce. Mr Edwards has sent a sheaf of corn; done in the old-fashioned way I remember as a child. This is the centrepiece. There are rosy, red apples, freshly picked, pears just turning a deep yellow, a bowl of autumn raspberries and so many vegetables. Caroline has washed Neville's potatoes and put them in a box covered in yellow tissue paper. Then she goes off to wash her hands.

"You never know where they have been," she says with a frown.

The vicar arrives along with lots of parents while the children wait excitedly looking at the stage. The Juniors open the service by singing 'Autumn Days' where we mustn't forget to say a great big thank you for all the things that autumn brings. I have my doubts as to how many jet planes they have seen re-fuelling, but they sing the words lustily without seeming to mind. They go on to sing about minnows darting down the stream and the frosted rings of the winter's moon, again seemingly without a worry.

Next, the Infants play their part by bringing their gifts to the 'stage'. It was Sara's suggestion, and it works beautifully. Each one brings a small offering; some present an apple (one with a bite out of it) or a pear. Others have brought small bunches of autumn flowers. Sara leads and they all follow. Everyone is rapt. It is then I hear the front door bang, James appears. He stands at the back and gives me a smile and a nod.

My class performs a little play about Ruth and Boaz. Emily is Ruth, gleaning the corn, and Peter acts as Boaz. Caroline is the mother-in-law, Naomi. In rehearsal, it was hard to get Peter and Emily to even hold hands let alone show that they were about to marry.

"I'll hold one of you, on one side, and one of you on the other," says Caroline, carefully placing herself between them and linking arms. Caroline's mum looks up at me and smiles.

"What are you going to do with all this?" asks James in a business-like manner, pointing to the produce, when the 'festival' was over.

"It has to go up to the church for a service tomorrow, then we will be distributing it to people in the parish."

"Do you need help with it?"

"Oh, thank you, James, but Peter's dad said that he would come over with a tractor and small trailer." He looks up at Sara, who has just popped into the hall. He smiles at her and his eyes twinkle. But Sara looks sad and distracted. Her hair is not its usual shining, smoothed curls. Her smile is half-hearted.

Mrs Field sparkles in with not a poly bag in sight. "Peter's dad is here, Miss Heron. Shall I tell him to wait?"

James replies, "Oh no, that's fine, thank you, Mrs Field, or can I call you Helen?" He twinkles again and I feel a twinge of jealousy.

Just then Sara bursts into tears. At first huge tears roll down her face, her mascara smudges as her body is wracked with huge sobs. She lowers her head, and her hair falls over her face. I put my arms round her and usher her into the kitchen.

"We'll make a start then," shouts James, taking control. "Right, now..." I close the door and turn to poor Sara.

"What is it?" I coax. "Are you ill?" She shakes her head; her hair is all over her face. "What is it then? What has happened?"

"It's Tim," she sobs, "he's, he's left me." Her words are almost drowned as she convulses into a paroxysm of weeping. I busy myself getting a cup of tea for us both.

"Is it just a tiff? Sometimes these things..."

"Oh, no... it's final, he...he told me." I can see that we are in for a long haul.

The next day Sara is late for school, it is not like her at all. But last night we did not leave until about nine and she had not stopped crying. Tim has given up his job and decided to travel the world, what is he thinking of? Poor Sara! Poor Miss Nelson without a teacher mid-term.

We are all in assembly and a swollen faced Sara arrives, immediately two of her children run up to her and hug her legs. She strokes their hair.

We get through the day. Thank goodness the afternoon is taken up by the church Harvest Festival. We sing 'We plough the fields...' and the vicar gives his sermon about sharing our food. The children then take the food from the altar and give it to members of the audience who they think will need it. I do not like to say, but I imagine most of them have donated the fruit or vegetables themselves, in the first place.

"Aww – look what she has given me."

"I've got a jar of home-made strawberry jam. How did he know that is my favourite?" They all leave, clutching their gifts and with big smiles on their faces.

At the end of the day, I hear the door bang, it is James.

"Thank you for your help..." I begin. He gives me a brief nod and marches straight to Sara's room. I leave them to it, there is a parcel that arrived this morning and I am intrigued to see what is inside. It is an alarm for little Eric, with a brief note from the Educational Psychologist, Andy.

'*You will be getting my report shortly, but the enclosed device should sort him out. Health Visitor to be contacted for reward system.*'

The 'enclosed' was a little pad that Eric must sleep on. It rings a bell if there is moisture. It will wake Eric who can then get up and go to the toilet. The nurse will bring some stars to put on a chart, for when he has done well. Surely there was more to it than that? Why was it happening in the first place?

Our School Nurse came the next day but to my dismay I realise that Aurora has not yet arrived.

"The nit nurse is here," I heard Neville hiss. Little Eric glanced warily sideways. He had already had to change into dry clothes this morning. He is, at last, manging to do this himself, thank goodness.

"Good morning, Miss Heron, I do not think that we have had the pleasure of meeting." The elderly, uniformed, pencil-thin nurse heads towards me. Her hand is held out and we shake. I can feel her bones crumple in her thin hand and so am careful not to squeeze too hard.

"I will inspect their heads while I am here, Miss Heron," she says. The children line up automatically, girls on one side, boys on the other. The 'nit nurse' in her navy uniform with hat to match stands in the corridor. She rifles through hair on obediently bowed heads. Every now and again one child is told to stand on her right-hand side. The others could sit back down. Eric and Emily have to stand next to her. Little Eric bursts into tears. Emily hugs Eric, and they are each given a letter to take home and a free bottle of 'corrective' shampoo. At break time Eric is asked to stay behind and the nurse gives him a talk about cleanliness. She shows him the star chart and the gold stars she would give him if she heard from his mother that he had been dry in the night. She would visit his mother weekly. He nods and clutches his little bottle of killer shampoo.

Eric's mum picked up the pad that night.

"I pray to God that it works. I don't know how I will manage if it doesn't when the new baby arrives." She sighs and waddles off. I do not like to ask when the big day is, but she looks as if she could give birth at any moment.

The report arrives the next day in a big fat envelope. It is a huge wad of notes to wade through. There is a covering note torn from a notepad.

'Vi, here are the results of my tests. No great underlying problems – except the wetting one. I thought that he may be ESN but his results show the opposite. Maybe if that baby is a big strapping lad, when it arrives, all will be well.'

His hardly legible name is scrawled across at the end. I pack the notes in my briefcase to read at home. I do not think I will find anything new there though, of course, I knew that Eric was not ESN – Educationally Sub Normal. His maths work is well above average as is his reading. His written work is within the norms.

October Sunday

Dear Dad,

I loved our Harvest Festivals – both the one in the school and one in the church. The children really threw themselves into the meaning of it all, the vicar was kind to do two services. Here, they know much more about growing crops and rearing animals, not like at my last school in Newford, where they were used to buying much more from the shops. I was a bit overwhelmed by the wonderful atmosphere and the part that the children played so well.

Our computer fund has not been growing fast enough, so Mr Shawell is now inviting people to a cheese and wine evening at Fish Hall where he lives, at £5 a ticket.

I have a little traveller girl in my class called Aurora. Her mother brings her to school, and she is always late. She is always sorry but just can't get here on time. I have asked them to come on time but, although she is very willing, they are always late. I decided to have a talk to the dad, and he said they would try harder. He said that all he wanted me to do was to teach Aurora about dreams. He said that dreams were essential to him. I can understand that I have dreamt for so long about being the Headteacher of a village school.

But then, this last Friday, Aurora was not in school and when I looked over the field from the car park, I saw that their caravan and truck had gone. I was so disappointed; she is a very clever girl and did well in most of the tests I gave the children. She was at the top for the intelligence test. I hoped that it wasn't me that put them off. Anyway, I needn't have worried because Peter's dad, who owns the field, told me that this is a regular event and that they will be back next year. I am looking forward to seeing her again.

I expect that your apples and pears are ready for picking and storing. I hope that your pickling is going well.

We will soon be putting our clocks back and the nights are drawing in, but I think that you will be busy in the garden for some time yet.

My fish are still coming up for pellets and I am feeding the birds, again, on my little shelf. So far, I have seen the robin and blue tits and great tits. I expect you have lots of birds of paradise, as always.

See you at half-term.

Love Vi xx

Chapter 23

Autumn half-term holiday

I have decided to buy a new car now and not wait any longer. I haven't saved enough but I can borrow the rest and pay it off over three years. I went to the garage I know in Newford. I have always used them and even though it is only a small business, I have relied on the mechanics there to keep my old one running, and they have never let me down.

I have chosen the new Mini-Metro. It is like my old Mini but is much more up to date and with a lot more space inside. There is even room for a radio if I want to buy one. The boot is unbelievably big, probably the right size for bringing all my marking home. But best of all is that I will not have much risk of it being unreliable and breaking down. I have become more and more scared of my old one, especially when I have been trying to get to school early or going up to Dad's. It often would not start, and I flooded the carburettor and had to let it stand for five minutes before trying again. I hope to collect my new car just before my journey up north at half-term.

At school, I must get going on the election of a new Parent Governor. We now have all the details of how to do this. To tell the truth, I have delayed until this term as there had been so much to do. I never seem to have a minute to spare, but I decide it is now or never. I show Mrs Plane how we want the voting slips worded.

"We didn't do this for Mr Norman, he chose Mrs Brown, and she has been most suitable."

"Well, I want it done differently now, Mrs Plane, the County Hall is very clear on the procedure and timing, which we must stick to." I try to sound firm. I do not feel it is right for me to simply pluck a parent out of the hat, so to speak. We live in a democracy and the parents must be able to vote fairly for their own representative.

Sure enough, at the last playtime of the day, the voting slips are all there on my desk. I hand Sara's out and count out my own. Each family is given two, one for each parent. I suddenly realise that we must be careful to make sure that if a family has more than one child, they do not get multiple voting slips. Mrs Plane has obviously thought of this too and the number is spot on.

At the end of the day, I give out the slips to my class. The children put them in their bags. The instructions are included, and votes must be in by the week after half-term. There is an extremely strict timetable.

Neville leaves his on the table. I run after him to the bike shed. He grabs it.

"Thanks Miss 'eron. I know who I'm voting for."

"It's not your vote, Neville..." I shout after him, but he has gone, pedalling from a stand-up position, whizzing off, not hearing me.

I wonder who will get most votes, I bet it is Mrs Buckingham, she always is so confident and seems to know everything. As I go back in, I bump into the Chief of Caretakers rushing out.

"Good afternoon, Miss Heron. I did try to contact you when I arrived, but you were otherwise occupied. I reported in at your office in accordance with regulations."

"Good afternoon, Mr Smith, have you managed to help Mrs Field with the heating system? Mrs Dunn was always in the boiler room trying to sort it all out, and with last year's winter in mind I wouldn't want anything to go wrong."

"Yes, indeed – it is all sorted now, I have updated Mrs Field on the mechanism. I must say I am pleased with my advice to you on the appointment of Helen. She is quick on the uptake and altogether pleasant."

"Yes, I think so too. But Mrs Dunn's heart was in the right place, she would have done anything for Fish school and the children."

"Sorry must dash, got another visit to make, Miss Heron."

Mrs Field is coming down the corridor smiling.

"All sorted, Mrs Field?"

"Yes, with the boiler, it all seems quite simple. There is an on off switch and if you want heating for a meeting, I can press an override switch."

"Mystery solved." I smile. It all does indeed sound so simple with no need to take a sharp intake of breath.

It is Mr Shawell's cheese and wine tonight. I really do not want to go but feel that I must, especially as he sent me a complimentary ticket. I wear one of my new dresses with a blue Maggie bow. It is green and navy and with matching navy high heels, I feel very smart. I make my way through the misty woodland road to The Hall. There is a huge lake to the right, and I wonder if this is where my heron comes from.

I turn off to a tree lined avenue and see ahead the dark shadow of what looks like a mansion looming. There are some big cars here already. I park near the exit to the drive, so that I can make a quick getaway.

In the huge entrance hall, someone takes my coat and points me through a doorway where there is a waiter with a tray of drinks. I take an orange juice and walk into the room crowded with strangers. They are all dressed very smartly; the men are in dark suits and the women in dresses that make mine look home-made. Mr Shawell comes over.

"Welcome, Miss Heron, so good of you to come." His plummy tones seem genuine enough. "Do come and meet Mrs Shawell," he ushers me over.

"Hello, come and sit down. Have you had some nibbles? How are you getting on at Fish school? I do apologise for not having invited you over for supper sooner." She smiles and I am pleased to see that her dress is quite ordinary, more ordinary than mine. She has not time, though, to wait for my answers, as she is busy rushing towards a new arrival, it is the vicar. I do not know anyone else here and am working out when I can decently slip away as I sink deeper into the pale golden velvet settee.

"Do you mind if I sit here?" It is a smart professional man with an easy manner and a twinkle in his eyes. I stare into his face and suddenly recognise him from my interview. He is the one from County Hall. I see him from time to time in the newspaper sitting next to our Chief Education Officer.

"How are you getting on? Now let me see it's a year now, isn't it?"

Before I have time to answer a man with a mayoral chain round his neck arrives.

"Ah the mayor of Newford. I didn't see that it said, 'Chains may be worn', on my invitation, did you?"

What is he talking about?

"It says that on formal invitations sometimes. I must dig mine out!"

"Oh, oh yes, I see."

"I hear from your voice a hint of a Yorkshire accent. Splendid county, splendid, indeed. And they have just completed the Humber Bridge, the longest single span in the world, so I hear. Now you will be in touch with the rest of the world."

He is speaking as if I still live in Yorkshire and am glad to be let out and escape by the bridge to Lincolnshire.

"I haven't yet found a reason to travel on it."

"I see. I see. But you have not answered my first question. How are you getting on at the school?"

"Oh, quite well, although it was difficult at first what with Mr Norman and everything." What am I saying? Why have I mentioned Mr Norman?

"It would be, it would be, in the circumstances." What circumstances? The fact that everyone loved him. Then I wonder if they appointed me because they knew I would be good for the children's education. The thought pleases me.

"Why did you appoint me?" I blurt the question without thinking, perhaps it is the orange juice.

"Well, we thought that a woman could best handle the situation. Mr Norman was an excellent headmaster, educationally, but we could not risk another scandal, could we? A steady hand and all that." His eyes dart.

Scandal, what scandal?

"So, you didn't appoint me because of my modern educational ideas?" I blurt again. He puts his hand on my knee and nods towards Mr Shawell who is standing up and tapping a spoon on his glass.

"Mr Mayor, ladies and gentlemen, welcome to The Hall and to our fund-raising event. Thank you all for your generosity. I can announce that we now have enough money to buy a computer for our school and the children of this parish will benefit from your money for generations to come. However, as citizens of this great country, we must also remember the children who are not so fortunate as ours here. In the circumstances, I have had a bowl placed at the door and I hope you will give generously. But please do not leave yet, there are so many nibbles left here, if you do not eat up my good lady wife and I will be putting on weight. Thank you all."

Polite laughs roam around the room as we clap gently.

My companion suddenly squeezes my shoulder. I wonder if he felt my foam shoulder pads.

"If you excuse me, I will slip off now, my dear. I have put in an appearance, and I must dash – early start tomorrow and all that. Keep up the good work." And with that I see him dodge though the crowds and disappear. As soon as I feel it is decent, I do the same.

December Sunday

Dear Dad,

Just a quick note because you will see me on Thursday as it's half-term. First, I will collect my new car and trade in my old one. I'll drive the new one around to get used to it for a day or two. Then I will come up to see you. I am so excited about it. What a relief for me to have a reliable car at last.

The new computer should arrive a few days after half-term. On Mr Shawell's advice I ordered it a while ago – he was so sure we would raise the money at his cheese and wine effort. I am looking forward to bringing Fish school up to date, at last. I have also been able to order a state-of-the-art trolley for it so that we can push it into the Infant room or the hall or wherever we need it. I imagine it will mostly stay in my room. I have a boy called Christopher who has played on his dad's computer at work, and he can't wait to use it.

We have a big trolley for our television already and that does the rounds into Miss Faye's class and into the hall. The TV trolley is taller than me and very wide based so that it does not topple. You know how heavy televisions are. I bet you remember sharing one with Uncle Sid's family next door. I remember you carrying it to our house every month and your knees buckling with the weight.

The computer trolley that I have chosen is lower than the TV trolley, of course, it is big, and it has lots of compartments and shelves.

What am I thinking of, going on about trolleys and school equipment? It is just that I am excited and I promise not to talk about them when I come to see you.

I have had all the paperwork about mother's gravestone. The stonemason sent it to me, as you asked, so that you did not have to trouble with it all. It will be a fine memorial to her and as it is granite it will keep clean for a long time. We can take a cloth if you want when we visit, just to be sure.

I bet your leeks and swedes need eating up. I am looking forward to making a stew and eating it with you. Then we will sit by the fire and have a good catch up.

See you Thursday.

Love Vi xx

I go to pick up my new car. What a day! I leave my old car on the forecourt and hand over the keys, without a glance sideways. My new car is in the showroom, it is gleaming blue, like a dream on a summer's day.

I sign all the documents and walk over with the salesman. I sit inside and put my feet on a paper mat to keep it clean, at least until I get out of the showroom. He leans in through the window and explains all the new switches. I turn the key, there are only four miles on the clock and the tank is a quarter full. I rev the engine. A smell of newness wafts up to me.

The salesman pulls open the big glass doors of the showroom and I slowly steer down the ramp and out to freedom. Suddenly, I do not know why now, I remember that I have left the hamster in the classroom. I try to reassure myself that it will be alright for a week, but what would the children think if it died? I suppose I could get another, and they may not notice. No, I will drive to the school and get it. It will be good practice for me.

On my way I think of Mam's headstone and the cost. Dad paid just over £500, just about what I have paid as the deposit for my car. I have been saving all my working life. Which is the best value? I wonder which is most needed. Which gives most comfort? I decide that there is no comparison, we need both.

Then, before I know it, I am off up north to see Dad with my heater full on, my old one did not work anymore, and I was always freezing. I can still smell that exciting newness.

I have the hamster, in its cage, on the back seat. I have wedged it as best I can, but it is fast asleep and seems oblivious to its long journey. We must travel no more than 50mph to run the car in safely. I tap my fingers on the steering wheel in frustration. The road ahead is clear, but I have been told not go over the correct speed until I have done at least 500 miles. It seems like a snail's pace.

Dad comes out as soon as I arrive.

"By gum, that looks good. I bet they stung you for it. Your mam's favourite colour was blue." He gets my case out of the boot after I have fiddled about with the lock. He carries the case indoors and I carry the cage with the, still sleeping, hamster.

That familiar comforting smell of home greets me again.

Dad is besotted by the hamster. He gets it clean water and puts the cage on a little table where he can see it and announces everything it does.

"He's looking up, he's having a drink." And, at night, I hear about every movement on the wheel. He is like a cricket commentator telling me that nothing much has happened yet.

"Why don't you get a pet, Dad? It would be a bit of company for you."

"No, I don't want one. It would be a great fuss for nothing."

The next day we go to the churchyard. Dad takes his spade as usual and, just in case the plot has sunk down, he takes a bucket full of soil from his garden. I try not to cringe as the mud spills onto the new carpet of my car. I think instead of what is important.

Gumbalding church is in a field with a soft track down to it. We bump along and park in the field.

We can see Mother's stone shining and bright above the moss-covered neighbours. I remember that she was always so shy and retiring. There is a rose tastefully engraved at the top right. It is a demure rose, so I think that is suitable, the engraving is cut and lined in dove grey enamel. Dad has got 'nothing but the best' for her and he is proud of that.

He tinkers about with the grass and soil for a while and then we stand there looking down. At the last minute we remember that Dad brought some flowers from the garden – Michaelmas daisies and a rose that has managed to hang on for this very moment. We stand again, looking down at them.

"Mebbie she is in the right place. Free from pain now, at peace," he says as we contemplate. Then he turns and walks quickly back to my mud-spattered car and home.

We watch the news. Maggie Thatcher is on telling us all how things will get better if we all try hard enough.

"What do you think of her, Dad?"

"I like her, from what I can tell. She seems to say what she means and stick to it."

"What do you think to a woman being in the top job?"

"I'm alright with women as long as they know what they are doing. I remember when they first had a woman for a vitinary. Mr Javelin, who was the top man, rang and asked me if I would mind a woman coming to inject cow against mastitis."

"What did you say?"

"I said that she could, and I wouldn't object, but she had to be up to the men."

"And was she?"

"I think so, I had no trouble with her anyway. Mr Javelin was glad I let her come, he told me after, because the other farmers would follow."

We do the same things as before. I shop and cook and clean a bit and Dad gets on with his garden. He brings in some carrots that he has stored in a box with sand and a swede from the garden. We have a stew and settle to a programme about the new Humber bridge.

"What do you think to the bridge, Dad?"

"It's alright, I don't need it, though."

"Do you remember when we went on holiday, we had to cross the Humber to go to Lincolnshire and we took the paddle steamer? It was the only way to cross in those days. Now, we could use the bridge, and anyone from Lincolnshire could do the same."

"Nothing good ever came from Lincisha."

"Maggie Thatcher did."

"Aye, there's always that." And he turns to me and there is a beginning of a spark in his eye that I have not seen for a long time.

Chapter 24

Fireworks

On my way to school, after half-term, I am driving along when I see the heron again. Huge handkerchief wings flap nonchalantly over the road. It suits my mood in my effortless new car.

The computer has arrived. Mrs Field has just taken delivery of it. There are three cardboard boxes, and one is huge. The trolley is here too, and it is almost blocking the entrance. I take off the corrugated card, taped round its frame, then wheel it into my room. It seems massive and does not sit comfortably anywhere. I move the television to the hall and fit the computer trolley in its space.

I am just sorting out the maths work when the phone rings. Its tone is urgent. I tell myself, again, that it always sounds the same but this morning it seems serious. It is Mr Pound, and he says that he wants to come and see me as soon as possible. This is interesting, I rarely get to see the husbands, they seem to leave early education to their wives. It is about his son's 'sums'.

"Come tonight," I urge. I do not want to be worrying about what he is going to say, I would rather get on with the query as soon as possible. The other aspect is, of course, that I do not want the parents worrying about their son either. When we have finalised the arrangements for the meeting, I bustle into Sara's room to ask her about David Pound's number work. I try to keep it business-like. I cannot deal with tears about her breakup with Tim in school time. She follows my lead.

"Oh, he's a lovely little boy, his work is great. I can't think why his dad wants to see you." She tries to smile but her eyes are still red and swollen.

"All the same, Sara, I'd better have a chat to David and look at his work. I'll send for him later."

The voting slips are drifting in slowly. I have put a box in both our classrooms, the children seem to enjoy posting them and peering through the slot to see how many there are. The deadline is the end of the week.

I am now expecting David's dad. I had seen David's work during the day and, although there was not a lot of it, I could not see a problem. I also sent for David and had a chat with him and gave him one or two mental arithmetic tests. He was fine and I saw no cause for concern.

I am sitting in my chair in the staffroom doing some office work when his dad and mum arrive. They are both huge people dwarfing me. I stand up to greet them. She is quiet and in a mousy brown coat, but he is boisterous and angry. He swaggers in with his hands in the pockets of his large corduroy jacket. He sits down immediately in an easy chair and leans back. Mrs Pound hesitatingly follows suit turning round to check the positioning of the chair.

"It's not very warm for the time of year, is it, Miss Heron?" says David's mother, I smile weakly. I really have not got time to be discussing the weather and want to get to the reason for the meeting.

"Now look," cuts in David's dad, as if reading my thoughts. "I believe in getting to the point, we are all busy people. I'm John Blunt me, I call a spade a spade." I sit looking at them both expectantly.

"Now, when I was at school, sums were sums and adds were adds. We knew what was what. It was alright when Mr Norman was here, we understood the sums."

But I still do not know what he is getting at.

"It's all fancy stuff now you've come to Fish. I said to Christine, let's take the bull by the horns and go and see the new Headmistress. Didn't I, Christine?" She purses her little red lips, almost hidden in her big round face, but she does not answer.

"I'm going to tell her, I said, didn't I, Chris? That's just me, straight to the point, take it or leave it. You get what you see with me."

He finishes with a flourish and throws his head back with his hair springing wildly about. Christine still does not move. She is balancing on the edge of the chair now and I cannot help worrying that it will tip up at any moment. I still have not got any idea what he is talking about. But, before I can politely enquire further, he starts talking again.

"Well, you wouldn't thank me if I didn't come and say it to your face, not like some I could mention."

This worries me as he seems to be implying that there are a lot of grumbles out there, but no one will tell me. At last, he pauses for breath, and I can intervene.

"Well. Mr Pound, I have looked at David's work and he seems to be getting along alright. Miss Faye has every confidence in his maths work. The mention of Miss Faye, though, proves to be disastrous and serves to move him away from the purpose of our meeting.

"That's another thing, when I was at school a teacher looked like a teacher not like a fashion model."

"Let's get back to David's maths, what exactly do you see as the problem?"

"Well, 'adds' should be adds and 'takes' should be takes, not this plus and subtraction rubbish."

Ah, I am beginning to see a glimmer of the difficulty and rush in hoping that I have assumed correctly.

"Well, you see, these days, we ask quite a lot more of the children. David will be expected to know that 'add' is the same as 'plus' and 'take' is the same as 'subtract'. You wouldn't want him to know less than the other children, would you?"

They are both quiet for a moment then he breaks the silence.

"Now what's this about rods stuff, anyway? The kid comes home going on about blue and white making an orange rod, well that's not sums to me, is it, Chris?"

"Ah, I see your concern. I have introduced these rods to teach the children about number bonds so that they don't need to keep adding using their fingers. Let me show you."

I take a box of the rods and spread them on the floor as my desk space is covered with notes and letters. I sit down on the floor tiles to show what I mean. To my surprise he gets up then moves down to join me. In no time at all he is making up sums, showing very clearly that he has a good grasp of number bonds and what I am trying to do. I look up at Chris, I am flushed with success.

"I never was good at maths at school," she says with an apologetic smile.

They are both silent, now, as I see them to the door.

"I'm good at maths and I can see our David is taking after me — goodnight, Miss Heron, thank you. I enjoyed that."

"Please keep in touch if you have any more worries," I call, as they get into their car. He smiles and waves.

Bonfire night is our next big event.

"The fire is always organised by Peter's dad and the PTA," says Mrs Plane. "They know what they are doing." So, we all relax and watch in amazement as the pile of hedge clippings has grown into a massive tower. James drops by, there is no smile for me today, maybe that is a good thing. I cannot afford to do what that Headmistress did and lose my job and it would be so easy with a man like James, I tell myself determinedly. I fear, though, that I am too late with this good advice to myself.

"Two things," he says. "Firstly, I'm worried about Sara, I will go and see her in a moment. Secondly, how are the plans for the bonfire going?"

"Everything seems to be going well, we are all looking forward to the big night. I try to play it down so that the children do not get too excited, though."

"Good plan, good. The PTA have all the food arrangements in hand." He looks down, takes a final drag on his cigarette, and dumps it in the metal waste bin. He rushes off down the corridor to see Sara. Something in the relationship is shifting.

I talk to children about rules for bonfire night and about the need to bring torches but no fireworks. I give strict instructions about coming with parents or older sibling. They shuffle about, I know they are finding it hard to concentrate amid the excitement. The dark nights seem to bring out a feverish anticipation of something magical about to happen.

It is the day before when Peter asks, "Have the fireworks come yet, Miss Heron?"

"What do you mean, Peter?"

"Well, when Mr Norman was here, he told us when they had arrived. I knew, anyway, because I saw him bring them in and put them in the staffroom. We always had a big display. You know like the ones in London. Well, not quite as big but you see them on the telly."

I go to the staffroom to see Mrs Plane. This cannot be true about the fireworks, surely? But Peter is a bright boy and would not get this wrong. I had assumed that the PTA did all the arrangements, including buying the fireworks.

"Mrs Plane, who normally buys the fireworks?"

"Oh, Mr Norman got them, he sent away for them, didn't you know? He was very generous, you know."

"How would I? Why didn't you say?"

"It's in the logbook. I know it is because we used to write it up together. I kept a diary and reminded him of the events, and he wrote them down in his beautiful script. I thought you had read the logbook." I had, of course, read some of the logbook but I certainly had not had time to trawl through all the past year, written with long flowing descriptions.

I march out because I am about to blow a fuse and that would not do a day before the fire.

And now here I am in Newford, buying fireworks. It is late and of course there is not much choice. I buy as many as I dare, I am not sure how much to spend and I do not know what is left in my bank account. I will get reimbursed, but I worry about being overdrawn.

I go home wondering why James did not tell me about buying the fireworks. He used to be so good at keeping me informed. I should have asked and not assumed the PTA were sorting it all. I should have checked. No time to worry about that now, I need to rest then do my best to make sure tomorrow evening is a success.

The parents have set out trestle tables and brought cooked jacket potatoes, with sausages and everything else you could want. They have borrowed the tea urn from the WI and are already serving hot drinks. Peter's mum and dad have set up lanterns, placed buckets of water at intervals and roped off the fire. There is a big old metal dolly tub filled with sand and a huge metal trunk for the fireworks.

"I'm afraid these are rather last minute..."

"Ah, there you are. Let's store them safely in here."

They barely cover the bottom of the trunk. How many did they have before I wonder? Did Mr Norman buy hundreds? If he ordered them in advance then he could have bought some of those that go on for a few minutes, those that you buy for an event. But I cannot dwell on these thoughts for long because I get swallowed up in the excitement and the dark and the torches and the food.

It seems as if all the village is here, there are even families I do not recognise all having fun. But I can't help worrying about the fireworks I have bought and hope they will not be damp squibs after last year's magnificent display.

Peter's dad does his best and I hear, 'Oo' and 'Aah', every time one is lit and shoots up into the air. They are not too bad, I think. Darren comes up to me with his face lit up into contrasts by his torch.

"Miss 'eron, this is good fun." He runs off and when I see him again, he is eating a big hot dog with red sauce all over his cheeks. I wonder fleetingly if he has come as Neville's older responsible sibling. But the thought goes out of my mind when suddenly, I am aware of someone near me. A presence like a shadow and a white vapour breath mingling with mine.

It is Mrs Plane wearing a dark mac and a black knitted hat, tied under her chin. She smiles gently and I can see her white even teeth. She stands next to me for a moment or two before moving off quietly.

There are a few more fireworks to go. I see Peter's dad hammering in a post. He puts one of the big Catherine wheels on and it lights up into a dazzling circle as it fizzes round and round. It seems to last for ages. And there are two more bigger ones to come as a finale. I had not realised how good these final fireworks would be. They are long lasting and give out a bright sparkling wheel image that stays in the night sky even after the final finishing bang.

"Wow!"

People begin to leave. I am sorry as I realise, for the first time, that Sara has not been. And come to think of it I have not seen James either. I wonder if little Sam is here with his mother, but I do not see her. I help the parents clear away, then it is all over. But I have one last thing to do. I go into the school feeling quite guilty as I switch the lights on and the 'monster' springs to life. I hear a creak and I swiftly turn; it is almost as if Mrs Dunn is still here and is going to complain and take a big intake of breath about the waste of electricity. I shiver and head for the staffroom. There is something I want to look up. I find the School Fund account book on the shelf above my desk. I have not bothered with it before and must think about raising money for it in the future. I turn the pages back to last year. October. Here it is. Just as I thought. I read in the ledger '£20 debit'. I follow the line with my finger 'fireworks'. I thought so. Mr Norman did not pay for the fireworks out of his own pocket, for some reason I got the wrong impression from Mrs Plane.

November Sunday

Dear Dad,

We had such a good bonfire at school. I was late buying the fireworks, but they went down well. The Catherine wheels were stunning at the end. We never liked them much as I remember from childhood. Maybe people still don't like them because I got the ones that were left over from the shop. Thankfully, they were huge and gave such a good show.

Do you remember our bonfires? You and Uncle Sid took loads of hedge cuttings into our paddock near the railway line to make a fantastic heap. You used to buy us a box of fireworks each from Ringham. I seem to remember that the boxes cost half a crown each. They had little Catherine wheels inside and we all just threw them into the fire to watch the fizzing and hear the banging. I used to play with them in bed, before the big day, and smell the grey gunpowder that trailed out onto the sheets.

But my best news is that we have had the computer delivered, at last. The cheese and wine party at The Hall helped raise the final amount of money. It is not my sort of thing as you know. I think that you are the same, we don't like a big fuss. But I met some interesting people, and it was all in a good cause.

I think that I have seen a heron flying over my garden. I hope that he has not noticed my goldfish. I know that you have bought a life size plastic heron to scare the real ones off. Maybe that is what I should have done.

Looking forward to seeing you at Christmas – not long now.

Love Vi xx

Chapter 25

Decisions

Mrs Field and I finished unpacking the computer early this morning. It is cream plastic and has IBM written in silver letters on the front of a blank screen with thick plastic all round, like a big picture frame. We manage to heave it onto the computer trolley and then there are two other boxes and lots of wires. It is all unknown to me and I have no idea what to do with the tape recorder or the typewriter board that has come with it. There is also a printer to complete the conglomeration. I wire up the electrical plugs with a screwdriver, but that is all I can do for now, other than ring the County Hall for help. Apparently, there is an adviser who lives nearby, and he will call sometime because he has a great interest in computers and has an idea of how to connect it up, which is rare knowledge.

The only instructions from the County Hall are that we must cover it when it is not in use. Mrs Plane was interested and at first, I thought she might knit a cover, but thankfully Caroline's mum has used two old curtains, which she washed and pressed, then stitched them together and put pieces in the side to shape it. It is like a tent with straight sides and a ridge roof. It's too big, but there our computer stands resplendent in its curious curtain cover. I suppose it stops anyone seeing the computer directly, but you could easily guess what the lumpy shape is under there.

It is pouring with rain today; it was lucky that we had a fine night for our bonfire. The children are still excited, and Neville has not arrived yet, which is most unusual for him.

Peter rushes in with his cheeks aglow. He is full of the success of his dad's bonfire.

"We had a clean burn, I stayed out with Dad and made sure every single twig was gone. I've been to have a look this morning and there is ash and it's still warm even with this rain. I saw Neville there just now."

"Thank you, Peter – it really was a very good bonfire."

"I hope none of the animals were frightened," says Christopher.

"Oh no, I saw to it that the ponies were in another field and the cats and dogs were inside." Peter answers as if he could not believe such a question could be asked of a farmer.

Neville arrives, he is dripping wet and covered in grey ash. Muddy black footprints follow him from the side door and down the corridor and into my classroom.

"Miss 'eron, look what I've got, right." He proffers his fists full of muddy wet, spent card cases of fireworks. Everyone looks to see his treasure, and for a moment, I am transported back to my childhood. I remember the thrill of the day after bonfire night when we went searching for spent firecrackers. The charred ends and the smell evoked thrill and danger. But I am brought back to the present by my class craning their eyes towards Neville. I hear the scraping of seats, and then speak quickly and sharply.

"Christopher, will you please find Mrs Field for me and ask her to bring a bucket?" Christopher gets up and dashes, importantly, down the corridor.

"Now, Neville, hand those over to me and go and get cleaned up. What are you thinking, bringing such dirty things into school?" He hands his treasure over, dumping his loot in my outstretched hands. I realise my mistake instantly, but Mrs Field is there with a bucket, and I drop them in. She smiles up at me and shrugs before going to get the mop. I have just finished washing my hands when I hear the door bang.

There are tripping footsteps down the corridor. The School Nurse peeps her head in.

"Can I have a word, dearie?" I settle the children and step into the corridor. "Mrs Edwards has had a baby boy. I have just been up there, and all seems to be well. Mr Edwards is so pleased of course. Another boy and this one is a bouncer weighing in at 9lb 9, so different from Eric who was very weak from the start."

"How is Eric getting along with his chart?"

"His what, dearie?"

"You remember his reward stars that you give hm for a dry night?"

"Oh, that yes, he's doing a bit better. If you ask me there is a lot going on there."

"Well, what do we do now?"

"That's it, all over. I keep giving him stars when he's done well. It is a proven method; don't worry, I'll keep an eye. There is nothing more we can do, and I am sure things will settle."

The November weather matches all our moods. It is dull and misty and then comes the first frost with my car skidding and doing zigzags on the lane. Thank goodness I bought the new car before the worst of the winter.

We plod on with our work looking forward to December and the cheer it brings with our celebrations. I do not think I will be hanging decorations from the ceiling in the hall, though. I will be hoping for an atmosphere that comes from the children and their ideas.

At the end of school, James strides in. He is wearing his smart grey suit and looks more handsome than ever. He perches on a bench in my classroom.

"I've got some news." He grins sheepishly.

What on earth can he be talking about? He looks so attractive, and I am wanting to go and sit on the bench to be with him. Suddenly, I want to smell his aftershave; I wonder if he has that spicey one on. Is his news about me? I hold my breath and stand frozen with longing.

"I have sold our house. I am over the moon. I can't tell you how pleased I am." He interrupts my thoughts.

"Sold your house?" I stammer. I wonder if he and Wendy are splitting up. My ideas are running away with me as I grapple to make sense of what he is saying.

209

"Yes," he leans back and hugs one knee. "Now all the worry is over."

"But I didn't even know it was for sale." I am so shocked.

"Oh, it's been for sale for over a year now. I am surprised that you didn't know. I was beginning to despair, but now, at last, I can relocate to Bristol to be with Mother."

He lights a cigarette and leans forward to blow the smoke casually into the classroom.

"Move to Bristol," I repeat inanely.

"Oh yes, it's all been arranged for some time – Mother's house is too big since Father died and her health is not good."

"But what about your job...?" I never did ask what he does.

"Oh, that's all arranged too, I'll be joining the family firm and eventually take it over. It's been on the cards for ages. It's just the house that has held me up."

At last, I sit down on the bench next to him and I can smell his aftershave; it is another new one and suddenly I feel nauseated.

"Don't say it. I know what you are thinking." James interrupts my thoughts.

"You do?"

"Oh, yes I can read you like a book."

"You can?"

"Yes. And yes, the people moving in do have children – three if I remember correctly. So, although you will lose Sam, your numbers in the school will not go down. I know that you always think of the school first."

"Oh, that's good," I manage to whisper, although numbers in school were the last thing on my mind. He eases himself off the bench.

"Must rush – lots to do. He stands to attention and gives me a mock salute. "I don't suppose I will see you again."

The next minute he is back, poking his head round my door with a grin.

"A word of advice – don't let that Mr Norman come to your Christmas assembly. Mrs Plane invited him in the summer, you know. I never could stand the man." Another quick salute and he is off again. What was I thinking? Well, I wasn't thinking, was I? This man is a real flirt, I have seen him eyeing Sara, and I should have known better. My fast-beating heart will catch up with my sensible brain soon.

I hear the door's final bang and his car revs up and swishes off up the lane.

Before I have had time to recover, I hear footsteps in the corridor. It is Neville and Darren.

"He 'asn't got you then?" Darren smiles cheekily. What is this young man thinking?

"What on earth do you mean, Darren?" I snap.

"That big fish, he 'asn't ate you?" He laughs.

"No, Darren, no I'm quite safe." We smile at each other and Neville interrupts impatiently.

"Miss 'eron, you know the 'amster, right? Well, who's going to look after him in the holidays?"

"I haven't thought about that yet, Neville, there is a lot to do before the holidays." I shoo them out and they head for the front door.

"Remember the front door is not for pupils, use the side door."

"I ain't a pupil but if I'm with Neville, I'll remember." Darren always has the last word, and he will not remember what I said, but he means no harm. They turn and head off for the side door. I get on with my marking.

Chapter 26

Moving on

I hear the front door bang; it is the adviser who lives nearby.

"Hello, I'm Mr Pratt, your friendly adviser. I come from Yorkshire like you, so we should get along famously, and I am also good with computers, as it happens." I am pleased to see him and relieved that he is not our area adviser. The children cope well with Mr Hall's name, but I am not sure about 'Pratt'.

Mr Pratt licks his lips and takes his jacket off. He rotates his shoulders and, staring fixedly at the machine, he rolls up his sleeves, just as if he is a consultant surgeon about to operate. His fingers twitch as he sets to work connecting wires and arranging all the bits and pieces. He stays there concentrating without speaking or looking sideways.

Eventually, he gets it all working. He shows how we can send a message so that a school, with a computer, even in London, can read it and reply when they have time to look. I am sure the children will like doing this, but I cannot really see the point. If we have a message, why don't we ring or write a letter?

"It is called a bulletin board," says Mr Pratt. "You will love it."

He stays late, fiddling about with programs and connectors before wheeling it all into Mrs Field's cupboard, for safety's sake.

"I hate to leave," he says. "I could stay with this machine all night."

I am so pleased that he does not. But I am also pleased that he has been, I intend to leave the machine exactly how he has set it up. All I will do in the morning, is wheel it into our classroom, plug it in and switch on. The wires and settings must not be moved. No one here would know what to do if anything is altered. No one must disturb it until Mr Pratt has some more spare time to help us further.

The next morning, I decide that it is time to sort the voting slips. Mrs Plane is here which I am pleased about.

"Mrs Plane, will you oversee the counting of the voting slips with me, please?"

"Mr Norman always did it all himself, he was good like that."

"It's not that I can't do it, Mrs Plane, but it is part of the democratic process there should always be more than one person to oversee the count. Then no one can cheat."

"Mr Norman would not cheat."

"Neither would I, but that is not the point."

She stands there whilst I sort the votes. Mr Pound is far and away the winner. I thought Mrs Buckingham would win, but she had only a handful of votes. I am pleased; he will be a good Governor and will not take things lying down, so to speak.

At home, the phone rings.

"Hello, Vi?"

"How are you?"

"Not too bad. How's that hamster?"

"He's doing well, gets on his wheel at night going round and round and getting nowhere."

"Don't we all?"

"He sleeps all day, so he does get a rest. Have you thought anymore about getting a pet yet? I am sure it would be a comfort to you."

"I've got ten."

"What?"

"Fish, I've bought some fish."

"But you've got some outside in your pond."

"Not anymore, the heron got them. I saw him early morning when I drew the curtains back. He took off like a big white sheet in front of my window and when I looked again, all my fish had gone. That plastic one I bought was no good at scaring him."

"Oh, what a shame."

"That's the way of things in nature. But watch out for your fish, you should net your pond as soon as you can."

"I will, Dad. But tell me about your new fish."

"Well, as soon as it happened, I got to thinking – it's no use only dwelling on the fish that have been eaten, I had to think of something else. It's not easy, but I had an idea. I went to that big garden centre at Ripsea, and they told me what to get."

"What did you buy?"

"I've bought a big tank and put it on that table of your mam's, the one she got from the sale room and did up. I've put a cloth on first because it'll be worth something, I bet. I've bought weed and a little bridge and coloured rocks as well as a pump and filter."

"That is so good – you can watch them swimming about."

"They do all sorts of other things – there's one with a bit of black on his tail and you can tell he's the boss and I watch him get the food first. There's a little one that hides away so I make sure I drop some flakes near him. I feed them every morning before I go out in the garden to do some digging."

"I am very pleased, Dad. I am looking forward to seeing them. What's happening in your garden?"

"I'm planting some more bulbs and I've bought some lily of the valley. Your mam liked them you know. She was a bit like them, beautiful but not boastful. By gum, she was beautiful. How's your vote going?"

"Very well, Mr Pound got in, I am pleased because he's the one that came in to complain about the maths I was doing in school, and he went away understanding all about it. He is a farmer and good at number work like you."

"Aye well, I had to be with farming – we had to make a profit. I wasn't good at book learning like your mam, but I did it all in my head. Ta-ra, I'm off to look at my fish."

The next morning, Sara pops her head into my room and is all smiles. Her arms are full of Christmas decorations and a little Christmas tree. She is wearing a red bobble hat and matching scarf over her long green coat. Her snowman tights add a touch of fun. I am so pleased to see her looking like this again, I wonder what has cheered her up.

"Oh Vi, can I have a word in the staffroom?" I'll just drop these off in my room then I'll be with you."

I make a tea for us both and bring the cups through.

"It's good news for me but I hope it won't upset you too much, Vi." She is quite her old self again.

"I have decided to leave my job here at Fish."

"Sara, think what you are saying. You have a good career, and you have all the qualities of an exceptionally good teacher. Consider your prospects," I urge. What is she doing? Mind you she would soon get another post and would certainly have an excellent reference from me.

"Tim has asked me to join him. He loves me, after all, and has found out that he can't live without me, we need each other so much. Isn't that wonderful?" Tears are running down her beautiful face, which I presume, by her smile, are tears of joy. Her mascara runs down her cheeks and she wipes it away with the back of her delicate hands.

"But I won't leave you in the lurch. Tim regrets how he left Miss Nelson. He told me to hand in my resignation now and then I can leave at Easter, without breaking my contract like he did."

"Sara, he is lucky to have you. I can see how much you love him."

"And he loves me."

"Of course."

"Poor you, Vi, everyone is leaving you. Thank goodness you will still have Mrs Plane. Beryl will look after you."

I am not sure about that, but I suddenly remember her gentle smile at our bonfire.

"She doesn't like change, Vi." Sara moves her head to one side and smiles sympathetically. "She will come round to your ways, in time, you will see. Her husband has only one thing on his mind and that is his farm. Mr Norman made her feel very special; you know I think she was a little in love with him."

Surely not? Is this the scandal? I hardly dare contemplate it and I rush off to my class.

Mrs Field has pushed the computer trolley back into my classroom. She has agreed to put it in my room every morning. Christopher gets going on it straight away. He seems a natural and soon he is stabbing away with one finger. He is writing a story.

Then suddenly there is an urgent shout.

"Miss Heron, the screen just went blank." Emily rushes over.

"You must have pressed the wrong button."

"I didn't, it just went blank; don't say I've lost all my morning's work."

"He has lost it," says Emily after scrutinising the screen and pressing some buttons. "He forgot to save it. You must save it, Christopher, every so often press 'save'."

"Leave it now, I will have a look at lunchtime," I say. But lunchtime comes and goes, and I am too busy.

That evening I sit at the computer; it takes me half an hour to find the program on the whirring tape recorder. Sadly, Christopher has, indeed, lost all his work on his story and will have to begin again.

I hear the door bang. Thank goodness it's Mr Pratt. He carefully takes his Harris tweed jacket off and rolls up his sleeves again. He rotates his shoulders and eyes his 'patient'. He works on a list of instructions for us. He begins with 'How to switch on and how to write stories'.

These notes will be useful, I think, as I set the printer going and it buzzes away leaving a pale dot message on the thin continuous pile of folded perforated paper.

"Thank you," I enthuse but I do not think he can hear me, never taking his eyes off the computer and fiddling about a bit with wires and the paper. "I don't know how I'd manage without you."

"You'd manage. A little bird tells me that you are doing well here in your first Headship."

"Who?" I am surprised but so pleased that maybe someone has noticed what I am doing.

"Ah, that would be telling." He eyes the computer again, with longing in his eyes, before switching off.

"I must dash, I've got to get my own supper ready tonight, Pat is out at the WI." He rushes away still unrolling his sleeves and carrying his jacket. "I'll be back soon."

It is the last week of term and the parents have arranged a Christmas party. The hall has been prepared with decorated tables. A team of mums have taken all morning while Sara and I have been trying to keep the children calm. Beth is helping, of course, and has incorporated the school lunch with party food.

At last, the children queue up and in we go. The younger ones tiptoe in first and then my class. There is an atmosphere of disbelief as we enter what seems like a dream world, like a fairy grotto of Christmas fantasy.

The PE equipment attached to the walls is decorated with tinsel and streamers. The tables have green and red cloths with a name place for each child. The food is cut into small pieces for children and placed in the centre of each table so that they can help themselves. Red jelly is in little green card dishes. There are presents and Christmas crackers and endless patience for the children's delight. The parents have worked so hard. But I suddenly see that Emily is crying, big silent tears are rolling down her face, and her shoulders are rising in deep sobs. I go over to her.

"What is it, Emily? What's the matter?"

"I keep thinking about the starving children on the other side of the world and here we are with too much. I can't eat anything because I keep thinking of them." And she sobs some more.

"I'll tell you what," I venture, trying to solve this problem so that it does not escalate. I do not want others crying so that all the hard work of the parents is spoilt. "Why don't we make a decision to raise money for the poorer countries in the world as soon as school starts next year?"

She brightens.

"Could I be in charge of the fund raising? My mum works for Oxfam, and we could send it through her."

"That's a very good idea, Emily."

"I'm looking forward to coming back to school in January already."

"So am I, Emily, so am I." We both smile.

After school I am in my classroom when I hear the door bang. I also hear the unmistakable heavy breathing of Miss Nelson. She is wearing a big coat and her hedgehog hat that I first saw at the swimming lesson.

"How nice to see you, Miss Nelson. Come into the staffroom and we'll have a cup of tea. No whisky left I am afraid." She looks at me and smiles tapping her pocket with one hand and the side of her nose with the other.

"What is your intake like this year?" I ask, I was not referring to alcohol and she knew what I meant as I continued. "Here, one family is leaving, and I believe we are having three more children moving into the catchment. There are two infants coming from the village."

I remind myself again that our funding depends on the number of children so I am pleased that our number on roll will not be going down.

"Oh, I haven't bothered, that's up to the next head but it seems that we have at least five to admit. Mind you, they are all littler and dafter than ever these days. Ha! Listen to me, they say heads should retire before disillusionment sets in. I think that I have left it too late."

"Do you know who will be taking up your post?"

"The Governors have appointed Mrs Goodman from the school in Newford where Mr Norman teaches. I never got to know him, but I hear he was very popular. Not easy for you, my dear."

"Oh, it has not really been a problem," I lie.

"Well, at Bridlypool, the Governors were keen to have a man in the school, so they have appointed Mr Daniels as the infant teacher, not a good idea in my opinion, but who wants that now? He comes from out of County, from down South, so I do not know how he will like being so far out in the country. But that's what the powers-that- be have decided."

She gets a flask out of her pocket and holds it up to me. I shake my head; I have more work to do before I can relax. She swigs from the neck of her little bottle.

"What's he like?"

"About your age my dear, and full of enthusiasm and new ideas like you. Good looking and divorced – which did not go down too well with the Governors, but it was her fault, not his, so that seemed to mollify them. You should go and see him some time, he will take up his post after Easter. Unattached and single..." she raises her eyebrows.

"I think I will, thank you." I am interested to see what he is like. We both know I will go.

"Now, I must leave you. Goodbye, my dear, it has been interesting to meet you, we must see each other sometime for a chat in the new year."

"We must do that, thank you."

We both know that we will not.

December Sunday

Dear Dad,

We have had a frost already and the whole garden was white over. Every morning I am pleased with my new car which will be so reliable in the winter. I expect your Brussels sprouts are coming on well for Christmas.

We are getting used to our computer, the children are doing a lot of story writing on it, and I have some arithmetic programs for them all to try. You'd be surprised how they take to it, even the younger children. I am in fear of pressing the wrong button, but they have no such qualms. We have it one week in my class and Miss Faye has it the next. There are also some games that the children like. One is a ping pong game, and they love that, but I don't think it is educational, so I limit that to play time. The

220

main thing is that they are all getting used to it. We are all learning as we go along.

We had a beautiful carol service led by the vicar in our church up the road, you would have liked it. Christopher and Emily were brave enough to sing the first verse of 'Once in Royal David's City'. They were a bit quiet, but everyone listened very carefully. We had some readings by the children from the Bible about the birth of Jesus. Caroline was especially clear as she had practised so well. They find it hard to speak up loud enough in a church where their voices disappear up into the rafters. The Infant class did a little Nativity play which went down well.

We are near the end of term now and it won't be long before I set off to be with you at Christmas.

See you soon, I'll bring the turkey.

Love Vi xx

It is all over, I have done a year at this school and survived. I remember the lecture I had at college, given by our principal. He told us about the importance of the job we were going to do. He began by saying, 'The first business of the teacher is to survive.' I have always remembered that.

At least I am still here and eventually found time to teach, I do not think I will ever be disillusioned enough to want to retire. But I have not shaken off the shadow of Mr Norman who is loved by all, except James, if you can count James now.

I pop into the kitchen to see Beth. She is all smiles even though she is stocktaking, and it must be boring and time-consuming. She puts the kettle on, and we sit together for a few moments.

"Have you heard from Mr Norman?" she asks. "I expected he would be at the end of term assembly; he so loved this school."

"No, I haven't heard from him. I asked Mrs Plane not to invite him in the circumstances."

"So, you've heard something then?"

"Yes, a little. I know that there was a scandal."

"Well yes, but it is still all hush-hush. He was so courteous and so good looking and a smart dresser at that." I am intrigued as she continues.

"It was his flamboyance we liked; he brought some colour to the school. It can get dull here you know with hardly anything going on." I would not say that, but I simply nodded not wanting to stop her flow.

"He was a loveable rogue; he didn't work like you do, but he got on with everyone." Not with James, I am thinking but then James would see him as competition.

"He loved the children and would do anything for them, you know."

"What was he up to, Beth?" I lean forwards. A frown comes over her face.

"Well, I don't suppose it will be any harm in telling you now. But we were advised not to say anything, nothing was ever said, and it is all over, I should think. But what I do know is that he was moved out of Fish school by the Authority. It was for his own good." I am thinking of Mrs Plane.

"What happened?" I am agog and I do not want her to stop now, especially as I have just heard the front door bang.

"We all kept quiet and it's water under the bridge now, but she should have known better what with her always sounding so posh and having little Jake in school. She got her claws into..." Beth stops, I know she has heard the door too.

It is Emily rushing in with Neville in tow.

"Miss Heron, sorry about using the front door, but Mum and Dad are waiting." She is out of breath.

"We haven't done anything about the hamster. I can't take him because we are all going away for Christmas, but Neville says that he can look after him for the first week and I can pick him up when I get back for the second week." Neville is standing there grinning.

"I'll take 'im 'ome if you want, right?"

"But Neville, are you sure? Have you asked your mum?"

"Oh, she won't mind. She won't even know. I'll 'ave 'im in my bedroom, right."

I hear someone coming through the side door. It is Darren. I am strangely pleased that he has remembered not to use the front door.

"Can we have the 'amster to stay for Christmas?" Darren asks. "And you know my toy racing track? Well, 'e can have a turn on that." Does he mean the poor hamster on the track? My mind boggles. I look at their eager faces. They are staring up at me and I am desperate. I do not want to be dragging the poor little creature up north with me again, especially in this cold weather. What am I to do?

"Alright, Neville, but take care of him, won't you?" They are all delighted, Neville grabs the cage while Darren takes the bag of food and some bedding. Emily thanks me and rushes off; her parents are waiting for her in the car.

"Can we use the front door, Miss 'eron?" says Neville and they both turn to me.

"Yes, just this once." I am pleased that they asked and go to the door to watch them.

The hamster cage is dangling on the handlebars. Darren is puffing along by the side while Neville stands on the pedals and races off at a great jerking speed. The cage with its little creature inside, is going up and down with every lurch of the bike.

I have a few days to wind down at home. Cathy and I go out for a meal to celebrate my year. I meet with some of my colleagues from my last school in Newford and we catch up and have a laugh. Joyce comes round for a chat and then I give Dad a call.

"Hello is that you?"

"Yes, Dad, I'm just ringing to let you know that I'm setting off tomorrow."

"By gum that's good, but I might be out."

"Why? Are you going to Mam's grave?"

"No, well yes, I'll see it, but I am meeting the vicar first, because I am going to be buying a new gate and posts for the churchyard. Did you notice how rotten they are?"

"No, I can't say that I have. Oh, just a minute I remember that little blue tit nesting there in a hole in the wood."

"Well, it'll have to find somewhere else now, but it will, there's a lot of old trees there."

"It's a good thing you are doing, Dad."

"Aye well, I'm doing something else as well."

"What's that?"

"I'm going to my sister's every morning for a mug of tea. I've started already and we have a good old talk for half an hour. She's nice company and I've been thinking that your mam would have wanted me to get out a bit more. How's that lad?"

"Neville? Oh, he's the same as ever. He has taken the hamster home to look after in the holidays."

"Good job you're not bringing it here, now I've got my fish and I haven't got time to look after it."

"Yes, I am a bit worried about how Neville took the hamster home, though."

"How was that?"

"The cage was on the handlebars of his bike, and as he pedalled it was swinging backwards and forwards, with the little creature clinging on for all he was worth."

"Same as us all. Same as us all," said Dad.

Vicky Turrell

Vicky grew up on a farm in East Yorkshire and after retiring from a career in education she has gone back to her roots living on a smallholding in Shropshire.

She has previously published two stories – It's *Not A Boy!* and *Me and my Mam*. This new book *Lessons with Dad* completes the trilogy.

You can hear Vicky read *It's Not A Boy!* on her YouTube channel – Countryside stories with Vicky Turrell

You can also read her columns from the Oswestry Advertizer and the Shropshire Star in her blog. blog.nestcottage.co.uk

Lessons with Dad